The Ambassadors of Elior and the Frozen Gate

Devin Anavitarte
Stephanie Wilczynski

Published in conjunction with the North American Division of
Seventh-day Adventists Youth and Young Adult Department

Printed in the United States of America

First Printing, 2020

Edited by AdventSource Publishing.
Creative direction, design, and illustrations
by Zemleduch Creative Studio

ISBN-13:

Dedicated to Esteban Deku, for showing us every day the character of the One True King.

Special thanks to Gabe Garcia for inspiring the character of Oliver and for assisting in the development of the world of Elior.

Special thanks to Jada Sails for assisting in the development of Mia and the world of Elior.

Chapter 1:
So, Bob is Crushing Me
Oliver

So, I'm sitting here on an airplane wondering why I am flying to Michigan of all places. I hate Michigan. Michigan is cold. It's random. It's stupid. Plus, I'm flying to my grandparents' house, and I haven't seen them in like five years. They speak Spanish and I don't. They try to stuff me full of *mofongo* and *pasteles* and I hate it all. I just want a hot dog. Do they have a hot dog? No. They don't have hot dogs.

"Hey, can you move your arm?"

"What?" I ask, removing my earbuds and looking at the man who is literally spilling into my seat.

"Can you move your arm?"

So, I move it. But I don't want to. I want him to disappear. I want him to somehow get sucked out the window. And then I realize if he gets sucked out the window, I probably will too, since I'm literally by the window, or I'd get smashed against the side of the plane or thrown into the large spinning thing that would chop me up into bits. Did I mention I hate flying? So, I move my arm.

"Can I get you anything?"

I look up to see the flight attendant who is staring down at me. I suddenly realize Bob, the dude beside me, has fallen asleep and is snoring.

"Can I have a new seat?"

"The plane is full, but I can get you a water."

I guess water substitutes being able to breathe in my seat. I nod and put my earbuds back in.

The flight from San Diego to Detroit was super boring, and

this one hasn't been any better. They really *should* do something special for unaccompanied flying minors. I read the pamphlet in the seat pocket about how to save myself if I'm dying about three hundred times, and I look at the shopping magazines, wondering who would ever buy anything like this. Tracy, my stepmother, probably would. She buys all kinds of things with my dad's money. But at least she stays home to take care of us, unlike my mom did, right before the divorce.

Now I'm flying to see my mom. I haven't seen her since last March during spring break. Mia, my sister, was supposed to come see us in San Diego last Christmas, but she chose to stay in Cedar Park. Whatever. I didn't really want to see her anyway. She's honestly really annoying. Obsessed with stupid causes like saving whales and trees and stuff.

I just want some new shoes. Dad promised I could have some if I spent the summer in Paradise with my mom and sister and grandparents. Oh, did I mention they live in a place called Paradise? Funny, right? The place I'm dreading is called *Paradise*. There's *maybe* thirty people there, a lake, a waterfall, some blueberries, and Mia. Great. I wonder what color her hair is this year. So here I am, clutching my water, the thing that will make me a happy Delta Airlines passenger.

The plane tilts and we're landing. I see a bunch of trees and water below me. It's so different from flying into California, with the big buildings and roads and smog and traffic. All I see are trees and water. Water in my hand. Water below me. Bob is breathing really hard, and I suddenly wonder if he hates flying too. He's definitely awake. I know because he is leaning over into my seat to get a peek out the window. Yay. I'm being crushed.

We hit some turbulence, but it doesn't freak me out too much. I'm used to flying, even though I hate it. I've been able to go on some pretty cool trips with Dad, Tracy, and Zoey. Zoey's pretty cool; she's three years old. Well, I guess she'll be four soon. At first I thought it would be kinda weird having a half-sister, but she makes me laugh, even though she calls me Olive, and I *hate* being called Olive. Oliver is just fine. And although I doubt she does it on purpose, I am anxious for her to learn how to really talk. We've been able to go to Cancun, NYC, and even London last summer. Dad's a history professor, so he gets usually summers off and travels a lot to study. They're already on their way to Alaska. I get to go to Michigan. So. Not. Fair.

"So, are you from around here?" Bob asks me, basically breathing on me. His breath smells like the turkey sandwich he was eating about forty minutes ago.

"I'm from San Diego," I respond, even though the last thing I feel like doing is talking to Bob. I actually don't even know his name. But he looks like a Bob. So, meet Bob.

"That's a long way from Kincheloe, Michigan."

"Yep," I respond, as I turn away, hoping he'll get the hint.

"I'm from Munuscong, right on the shores of Munuscong Lake."

I nod, turning up the volume on my phone, as *Circles* by Post Malone plays louder.

Now they're asking me to put my device away because we're about to land, but I ignore them because I'm pretty sure a fifteen-year-old's iPhone isn't going to crash our plane.

I look down and see Bob's really sweaty hands gripping both armrests really hard, which leaves me with only one and the window.

Landing is kinda bumpy as Delta flight 1255 arrives at Chippewa International Airport, which is basically a lump by some trees in a field. It only has one terminal and I wonder why they even built this place. Probably to torture half Puerto Rican, half white teenagers like me.

Yay. We're alive. I immediately look at my phone and the thirty text messages I've received from Courtney.

U take off?

Jennifer is getting on my nerves

Imy :/

Have you landed?

Hey my mom bought season passes to Disneyland, ask your dad if its cool to buy you one

Then there were a few pictures of her food from lunch, a couple selfies with her friends Becky and Jazmin, and an *ily come home now!*

I respond with *landed*, and figure I'll call her later.

Yeah. Courtney. So I like her. She is cute or whatever. Blonde girl from Cali. She's about two months older than me. But I dunno. She can be kind of dramatic, especially when she's with her friends. But all the other guys on the team have someone. And we're all friends. So, yeah, meet Courtney. I'll call her later. Maybe.

I'm in the back of the plane, and Bob isn't going anywhere anytime soon, and I'm wishing I could jump out the window. I see the guys with orange vests pull up outside the plane and start unloading our bags. I'm hoping mine is there. Tracy lost her luggage once in NYC. It wasn't pretty, but Dad bought her all new clothes, so she ended up being just fine. Honestly, with her parents' money, she could have bought them herself. My step-grandparents are loaded.

Of course, everyone is taking their sweet time leaving the plane. And I can't decide what is worse – sitting here next to Bob, or the awkward car ride I'm about to take to "Paradise" with Mia and my mom.

"Well, I hope you enjoy your summer," Bob smiles at me.

I turn my music up louder.

Eventually I leave the plane. I have my backpack and I find myself at baggage claim. My bag is red, and I'm not seeing it. Well, to be clear, I'm seeing a lot of red bags, and none of them are mine. I mean, the plane wasn't very big to begin with. Why are there so many bags? Bob lugs his bag away. For such a big guy, his bag is super tiny. I smile to myself.

My phone is vibrating. It's Courtney. I ignore it.

Okay, I know I'm sounding like a jerk, but please understand I'm about to have a terrible summer. I mean, I don't need too much to be happy. Give me a soccer ball, my PS4, some Doritos, a nice nap and I'll be good. It's just that the last time I was with Mia things didn't go very well. Plus, my mom...she...well, it's hard to put into words. I mean, a lot of kids go through divorce, so I'm not being dramatic or anything. I just think it takes a lot of energy to be around them, and I'd love just a few days on my own. But the school year just ended, and I'm already in Michigan. I haven't seen my grandparents since before the divorce. I mean, they've invited me up here. I just...I dunno. It's complicated. They're on Mom's side. Dad's parents are dead, so no one is on his side. Just Tracy and me, and Zoey who is way too little to understand things. Dad's not the bad guy in this. So, I didn't come up to visit. Never mind. It's complicated, okay?

My phone buzzes again. I look down. Mom.

We're outside. Can't wait to see you.

I respond. *Still waiting for bag.*

And as I look up, I see some kid grabbing it. I know it's mine because I put a bracelet around it that Courtney made me at Winter Bible Camp.

"Hey, that's mine," I say, approaching the kid.

"Nu uh!" he snaps back, pulling my bag away.

"Dude, check the tag."

"Mine," the kid hisses as his mom approaches.

"Danny, that's not yours," she says, smiling at me. "Put it back. Sorry about that."

Yeah, Danny, put it back. I don't say anything. I just look at him. I'm nearly two heads taller than he is. And then he literally just drops the handle and the bag flops on the floor. He laughs and is pulled away by his mom.

Dude. Michigan is the worst.

I grab my bag and go outside, and it's way cooler than it was earlier this morning in Cali. How do people live up here? I see my mom waving me over from the silver Toyota Yaris parked by the curb. She immediately gets out and runs over to me. She squeezes me into a hug, and I'm immediately reminded of coming home from school to the smell of *tostones* frying in the kitchen and the sound of her voice singing and laughing, and I realized I missed her a lot more than I thought I did.

"Hi, Mom," I say, hugging her back.

"You're so tall, *Mijo*," she says, kissing my forehead. It's weird because I'm taller than her now, and I never was before.

"Yeah, I guess I am," I grin, standing up a little bit straighter.

"Was your flight okay?" she asks, taking my bag.

I let her, as I follow her over to the car. I can see my grandpa in the driver's seat.

13

"Yeah. I guess."

"Good. Are you hungry?" she asks.

"Yeah."

"I'm sure Lita and Mia are cooking up something wonderful," she says, putting her arm around my waist.

I'm relieved Mia isn't in the backseat. I wasn't looking forward to being crammed next to her for however long the ride would be. I decide I prefer Bob.

"Are we far from the house?"

"About an hour," she answers, as the trunk pops open. I let her put my bag into it. I know I should probably do it myself, but there's something nice about seeing my mom actually do something for me, instead of doing everything for Mia. *Ugh. Mia.*

I watch the driver's door open, and there's my grandpa stepping out just as I remember him. Well, I guess a little older. A little smaller. Same smell, I realize as he hugs me. I guess it's his cologne.

"*Hola, nieto,*" he says.

"Hey, Grandpa."

So, I used to call him Lito, but something in me doesn't want to call him that. It's been too long, and my Spanish has definitely left me. I don't really feel a need for it anymore.

I can tell they're both happy to see me, and then something in me shifts. I can't explain it. But I suddenly feel like I don't belong here, and I really shouldn't be here, and they don't really know me, and I wish I was playing soccer with Rodrigo and Abel or just hanging out at Courtney's house. I look down and pull out my phone. I text Courtney.

Miss you too.

"Can we stop at Sonic?" I ask as I get into the car.

"*Mijo,* Lita is cooking. Can you wait till we get home?" she asks.

"Fine," I mumble as the car drives away from the airport. I fight every urge to put my earbuds in as the questions begin to hit me in the face like raindrops.

How was my year? *Fine.*

Did I get good grades? *I guess.*

What did I learn in school? *Nothing really.*

Am I dating anyone? *No.* I lie.

How's soccer? *Fine.*

Am I the best on the team? *Yeah.* I lie. I'm basically average, which is really annoying, because I try really hard but can't seem to be as good as a lot of the other guys.

It's the longest hour of my life. Michigan is just as boring as I remember. There are barely any buildings and I kind of miss the traffic. It's way too quiet. Way too cold. Way too...empty.

Kind of like how I'm feeling inside.

This is going to be the longest summer of my life.

If she hadn't ruined things with my dad, she would know all of this stuff about me anyway.

Between all the questions, my grandpa makes little side comments to my mom in Spanish, and I have no idea what they're saying. They're probably talking about me.

Maybe Bob can find me and free me.

Maybe.

Eventually I put my earbuds in and ignore them, staring out the window as the world fades away.

Chapter 1
Study Questions

1. What stands out to you about Oliver's personality?

2. Read James 1:19-20. How could the way Oliver responds to Bob, the little boy in the airport terminal, his mother, and his grandfather improve if Oliver took this advice?

3. Sometimes trials happen in life, like divorce and separation. What passages from James chapter 1 could you use to bring encouragement to someone who is hurting from these types of challenges?

4. Why could there be such tension between Oliver and his sister Mia?

5. Oliver mentions at the end of the chapter that he feels empty inside. Have you ever felt the same way? God didn't create us to feel this way. Where do these types of feelings come from?

6. Read James 1:16-18. What do these passages tell us about who God is? How could these words help Oliver's mindset?

Chapter 2
So, I Have to Share My Basement
Mia

"*Mijita*, is the *mofongo* ready?"

I give the gooey (I don't think it's supposed to be gooey, why is it gooey?) substance one more whack with the mallet and stare at it skeptically. I then shrug at Lita. "I don't get how we ended up stuck in the kitchen making dinner while the man of the house gets to do something else. What is this, 1955?"

We're standing in a kitchen that very well may be from 1955. The house is cozy enough, and smells like all grandparents' houses seem to smell, though the smell of plantains is currently taking over my senses.

Lita steps away from the *arroz y gandules* to inspect my project. She is thin and small, but not frail, and her warm hand around my waist makes me feel safe. She gasps. "*Dios mio,*" she mutters. She catches my glare and decides, "It will taste fine, and that's what matters."

I somehow doubt it will even taste fine, but I don't really care. I have no urge to prove myself in the kitchen. Plus, I don't get why we have to roll out the red carpet for Oliver. Did Mami and I get homemade Puerto Rican specialty dishes when we arrived at Lito and Lita's house yesterday? Try some fast food place called Culver's. From what I can tell, it's a popular fast food chain in the Midwest. I haven't seen any back home in Texas. And the food was okay, but it's not like it was Whataburger. And that isn't the point, anyway.

The point is that Oliver isn't even going to care.

"Why are we going out of our way for that kid?"

Lita smacks me with her wooden spoon. "Mia, that kid is your brother, and none of us have seen him in a long time. We want to make him feel welcome."

I look one more time at my blob of *mofongo* and decide that it kind of resembles my older brother a bit. "Speak for yourself."

"And may I remind you that you decided not to go to the airport to pick him up. Don't insult your abuelo. He makes the best mofongo you ever tasted. And gives the best kisses."

Did I mention my grandparents are madly in love? My grandfather, Lito, was born in Michigan, probably not far from here, but his parents raised him in Puerto Rico, where they were originally from. My grandmother, Lita, spent her whole life on the island until she married Lito after college. They moved to Michigan with Lito's parents. Why does my family have an affinity for the frigid cold? Nobody knows. I bet there are some discrimination stories about a Puerto Rican family living in a predominantly white area. My mom, who spent most summers in Puerto Rico growing up, moved down south as soon as she could.

Oh, and also, their names aren't Lito and Lita. It's just short for *abuelito* and *abuelita*. I spent the first ten years of my life thinking Lito conveniently married someone with the girl version of his name.

I hear a car pull into the driveway at the same time Estrellita, the caramel colored pom terrier, starts barking her little head off. My heartbeat quickens. They're here.

I'm rooted to the spot when the door opens, and in walks the prodigal son. He's taller than the last time I saw him, which was more than a year ago. Where I favor my mom's darker complexion, everything about Oliver screams "white boy," from the green eyes to the light skin (though he can get pretty tan in the summer). He has dark hair, but so does my father of ambiguously European descent. I'm just the opposite. I may have darker skin, but my natural hair is lighter, and I have hazel eyes. Nobody would peg us as siblings, or probably even first cousins. See? We have nothing in common. Not even the way we look.

"Oliver! Come in, come in. *Déjame mirarte*," Lita says as she pulls him in for a hug. "*Ya eres un adulto. Y tan guapo!*" Oliver awkwardly sets down his suitcase and makes a smile that comes off as a cringe. The dog growls at him, and Lita picks her up.

"What?" he asks uncertainly.

"She says you look tall," I explain. It's not exactly true, but

I'm not about to tell him that he looks grown up and handsome.

"Okay," he says.

I see my mom trying to catch my eye. She knocks her head toward Oliver and raises her eyebrows. She's telling me to say hi, or else.

"Hi, Oliver."

"Hey, Mia."

I just kind of stare at him. He just kind of stares back. And this is it. He says two words to me and all the hurt comes flooding back, threatening to knock me to the floor. Our parents split up five years ago, but that was the okay part. It was the months leading up to it with the arguing and the screaming and the slamming doors that was the worst. And my brother and I, stuck in the middle, did what you're not supposed to do. We took sides.

"Anybody hungry?" Lita asks, trying to cut the tension with conversation.

"Starving," Mami says gratefully.

"Do I just leave my stuff on the floor, or..." Oliver shrugs.

"You'll be in the basement with Mia," Mami points to the door to the side of the kitchen. "Just like when you were little."

"I don't get my own room?" Oliver looks queasy, like that one time I was forced to go to Disneyland with Oliver and my dad and his new wife and Oliver spun us way too fast on the teacup ride.

"There are only two bedrooms. Be thankful you're not sleeping on the roof," I snap. He doesn't need to know that I'm repeating the exact words Mami snapped at me two nights ago when I complained about sharing my space in the basement.

Oliver takes his stuff downstairs and then we all sit around the dinner table. While Oliver scoops some questionable *mofongo* onto his plate and sniffs it suspiciously, I lean over to Mami who sits on my right. "How was the car ride? Awkward?"

"It was fine," she assures me. "It's going to be a great summer, you'll see." She's trying so hard to pretend everything is perfect. But I know her. Back home in Cedar Park, it's just the two of us. We moved there after the divorce, so nobody has met my dad, and only a few have even met Oliver. I try not to talk about them much. They aren't part of the family anymore. And, sure, Mami and I fight plenty, but we're two strong-willed women, and I wouldn't have it any other way. Even though I lost the battle about the basement.

I start to dig into my food and catch Oliver glaring at me from across the table. "What?"

"We haven't prayed yet."

"So?"

Lito clears his throat. "You're right, Oliver, let's all bow our heads for prayer. *Querido Padre que estás en los cielos…*" and he launches into a lengthy prayer. I tune out immediately. Now, I'm not saying God isn't real. I spent enough time in Sabbath school as a little kid to realize that the world probably didn't just accidentally pop into existence. But I've also seen enough of the way Christians treat people who are different than them to decide that I don't want any part of them. So I sit still with my eyes open, right hand holding the fork halfway to my mouth, and I watch them. Lito looks like he really believes what he's saying. Lita squeezes his hand tightly and mutters, "*Sí, Padre,*" every few seconds. Oliver's eyes are squeezed tight, and he is literally making prayer hands with his elbows on the table. I remember being dragged to church with Dad and Tracy every time I was forced to visit them in San Diego. Plus, he's spent the last year as a freshman at San Diego Academy, so he's been indoctrinated pretty badly. Who knows what kinds of lies are filling his gullible head? And then I see Mami sitting rigidly beside me. She's being respectful, I know, something she always does when we visit Michigan. She'll dutifully play the part of the good Christian daughter as if the church didn't completely abandon her when she was getting divorced. Her head is bowed, but I see her eyes open, too. Tears gather at the edges of her eyes, but she quickly swats them away. I look away before she notices I was watching.

Dinner goes about as badly as I am expecting. The questions revolve around Oliver, and what's been going on in his life, though he somehow manages to constantly have his mouth full of food, which stunts each attempt at conversation. And I know the food isn't that great. I'm mostly quiet, only piping in to impatiently translate for Oliver when he gets lost in the Spanish. He used to be fluent, but I guess that's just part of the old life he threw away. Like Mami. And me.

Then, it's time for bed. Mami kisses me goodnight, and says, "Sleep well tonight," a phrase that sounds more like a threat than a loving promise.

She takes a step toward Oliver who abruptly backs down the stairs. "See you tomorrow," he utters.

She nods her head. "I'm glad you're here, Son."

But he's already popped in his earbuds.

By the time I brush my teeth, change into my Rosie the Riveter pajamas, and head down the stairs, Oliver has already made himself comfortable in bed. My bed.

"That's mine," I say curtly. I gesture to the deflated air mattress in the corner. "That's yours."

He takes his earbuds out but makes no move to get out of the bed. He's playing a game on his phone. "Your hair is purple."

My hair is long and hangs in waves nearly to my waste. And yeah, it's purple.

"I don't need to conform to society's standards of beauty."

"And yet you're wearing makeup." Okay, don't judge me. 8th grade can be a warzone.

"Thanks for not remembering my graduation."

"8th grade is nothing. You'll see when you're in high school."

"You were really rude tonight."

Oliver sets his phone down and sits up. "Mmmk, Mia. Stop acting like you don't mope around every time you're forced to visit Dad and Tracy. Back when you used to visit."

So, it was me who stopped the agreement. When Oliver and Dad moved to San Diego, it was agreed that we would take turns visiting twice a year. I would go spring break, and he would come Christmas. The next year it was reversed. But I didn't want to go for Christmas last year because I couldn't stand spending another holiday where everything was focused on Zoey, my Dad's replacement daughter, and on Oliver, the perfect firstborn. They have a full, white, family unit thing going on, and I was always the odd one out. The consequence, though, was that Oliver didn't come for spring break and it's all my fault that Mami hasn't seen him in over a year.

"You're right," I say nonchalantly, though I'm boiling inside. "I don't want you here. But, for some reason, Mami really does. So, how about we just leave each other alone this summer, and just get through it, and then we don't have to see each other again for a long time. Deal?"

"That's been my plan all along," Oliver sighs as he leans back on the pillow and resumes his game.

"Glad we're on the same page."

"Great."

I remain standing by the bed, arms crossed in front of me. He gives me half a glance. "I'm not getting out of the bed."

Then, I remember something. "The bed is yours," I consent. I air up the mattress and pull out a musty sheet and pillow from the closet. I'm already pretending to be asleep by the time Oliver tries to plug in his phone to charge and realizes the only wall outlet is across the room. Away from the bed. Right next to me.

I grin to myself, but my stomach is still twisted, and I wonder how I am going to make it through this summer.

Chapter 2
Study Questions

1. What stands out to you about Mia's personality?

2. Read Hebrews 3:12-14. What is Mia's perspective on the way Christians treat each other? Have you ever been hurt by someone who claims to be a Christian?

3. Mia feels like she doesn't fit in with her father's new family. Have you ever felt like you didn't fit in somewhere? Read Hebrews 2:5-14. How might Jesus have felt when He walked among us?

4. Mia and Oliver decide to ignore each other in order to get through the summer. Is indifference worse than anger? Why or why not?

Chapter 3:
So, the Puffy Rat-Dog is Fast Oliver

I kick a pinecone as a bird flies above me. I mean, I guess it's kind of nice out here, if you like this kind of thing. Fresh air. Big trees. Waterfalls. We heard the guy talk about the falls. There are high falls and there are low falls. I don't care about the waterfalls. But boy, aren't Gramps and Grams totally sold on them? They made us take a tour of them, and we heard a bunch of random facts that I'm not even going to get into.

I've been in Paradise, Michigan for about two weeks now, and I can't shake from my head the "Glad You Made It" sign posted at the front of the town as we drove in. Then Gramps had the "solid" idea of taking everyone camping. There's this state park about ten miles away from the house and the major attractions inside are these big waterfalls. I had to look up the spelling because I honestly can't even pronounce it, but I guess I'll take a whack at it: Tahquamenon Falls State Park. There, I said it.

So, they pulled out the old pop-up camper and a tent, and guess who gets to sleep in the tent. We've been camping since Thursday night, and it's currently Sunday. Oh, I forgot to mention, the first thing I did after my first night in the basement was to buy a long extension cord so I could charge my phone. My phone is the only thing that has kept me sane. The internet is weird and slow and it's been just a bunch of touring "Pure Michigan" with the family and old movies and weird food. And now we're camping.

I'm currently at the picnic table and thank God for that portable charger Tracy bought me, because I'm playing a game on my phone, attempting to block out the noise from the small puffy rat-dog that hates me. I don't know what her deal is, but she always barks and growls at me. Her name is Estrellita which apparently means "little star" in Spanish, which I refuse to call her, so we'll go with Pluto, because Pluto is also a dog and a dwarf planet, and planets and stars are kind of the same thing, right? Mia was sure to "educate" me that the dog is a girl, and Pluto is a boy's name, but it honestly just makes me want to take the rat-dog's collar off and replace it with one that says Pluto.

"Pluto. Quit it!" I call over as she barks at a tree. If she thinks the squirrel she's annoying will go down lightly, she's definitely wrong. I'm pretty sure that squirrel could tear her to shreds.

"*Flaco*, walk with me." Gramps catches me off guard. For an old dude he moves like a ninja and is pretty strong. Watching him set up the pop-up camper was dope. I shoulda probably helped him, but I'm on vacation. And what is *Flaco*? I'm immediately looking it up on my iPhone. Skinny. *Wow*. Okay, Gramps. I've been lifting, even if he doesn't see it.

As much as I don't want to be alone with him or talk to anyone, I see my Mom appear in the doorway of the camper and the look on her face means I better do what he says if I want to survive the night, so now I'm walking with Gramps. I can tell how much he loves it here.

"It's *hermoso*, *Mijo*, isn't it?" he asks.

I take one earbud out as we walk. I'm not going to completely tune him out. I'm not a total jerk. "You come out here a lot?"

"As much as we can. It's God's country."

"There are some nice hiking spots in Cali too. I really like it there. There's the beach and mountains all in one place."

"I've never been."

"You should come on vacation. Go to Six Flags. You like roller coasters?"

"Very much."

And I'm imagining the old guy on the Tatsu, my favorite ride at Magic Mountain, and thinking he's a pretty cool dude.

"What kind of man do you want to be?" he asks me, and I realize he's taken me out here to have that "deep" conversation I try to avoid every minute of my life. People spend so much of their time being overly serious, and I feel like it's not that deep, and everyone can just take a chill pill and things will mostly work out fine. But I see that look in his eyes and he's waiting for my response. I feel the pressure to say something that will impress him, so I do what I do best: impress.

"Someone that finds their true purpose and points people to God," I say, which is something my Bible teacher would want me to say, something I've said to him before in an essay. I got an A on that essay. I get good grades. I try really hard. I want to do it right, you know? Have a good job, a good family. These things are important. So, I'm going to do well on my SAT and keep my grades up.

"*Nieto*, that's the most important thing you can do. I'm proud of you." And I can tell he really means it.

"Thanks," I say. Yeah, I'm on the right track. I always go to church. I'm learning guitar, well, a couple chords here and there. I've played for song service for chapel and Sabbath school a couple times. I think it's important to be good at a lot of things, you know?

We talk some more, but not about anything really important or too heavy, and before I know it, the time has gone by pretty fast, and it wasn't too bad. Suddenly we're standing before the camper again and my mom is stepping out of it. Immediately she grabs my arm and pulls me by a tree and it kinda hurts, and I can tell she's not too happy with me.

"Ow," I say, pulling away from her reach.

"Give them to me," she says, extending her hand in my face.

"What?" I ask, kind of annoyed.

"Your headphones. *Now.*" When she says now her accent flares up, and I can tell she's being serious.

However, I'm stubborn like her. Afterall, I'm her kid. "Why?'

"Because you've been wearing them for two weeks straight, and your Lito is trying to spend time with you, and you can't even give him a *moment* without them." There's her hand again, in my face. "Now," she repeats.

And so I'm rolling my eyes and sighing extra loud as I fling them over to her. She only catches one of the buds; the other one hangs down toward the ground. I couldn't find my Air Pods before I left San Diego. I glare at her.

26

"What's up with you? You've been moping around for two weeks." Her hands are now on her hips. Another bad sign. But I can't help myself.

"Nothing," I snap as I start to walk away.

"If you walk away right now, you better keep walking into the woods, because you're *not* coming home with *me, Mocoso*."

I keep walking. It's better than what I want to do. I want to turn around and blurt out in her face all the words that I've bottled up for years. I want to tell her she's selfish. She's dramatic. It's her fault they're divorced. That I know the truth. I know she loves Mia more. But instead, I keep walking.

Okay, so I know that whole thing escalated quickly, and that it was kind of dramatic, but Mom and I haven't really fought in years, and there's a lot that needs to be said that if I told her would really hurt her. Sometimes it's better to just say nothing. She thinks I've been moping? I'll show her moping. I'm walking through the woods, and I have no idea where I'm at or where I'm going, I just know I want to get out of here. I want to get away from these stupid trees and the birds and all this disgusting fresh air. Give me my smog, please.

I don't know how long I walk, or how far I go. I know I'm not near any of the campsites anymore, and I'm nowhere near the main waterfalls. I'm just somewhere in the woods, and then of course there's Mia sitting on a blanket by a log with Pluto tied up to a tree, and of course Pluto is barking her head off at me. Mia looks up from the journal she's writing in, and stares at me. Come on, Mia, you can't even let me have a random forest. Do you literally have to be *everywhere?*

"Are you following me or something?" she immediately asks.

"No," I snap, turning away. There has to be somewhere I can go.

"Okay, *adios*," she mutters, lying back down.

It stops me. And I don't know if it's because she threw Spanish in my face, or if it's the way she looked at me, or just because I'm mad about my headphones, or the fact that I'm in Michigan in the first place, but I call her a name, and it's not a very nice name, and before she can say anything back, I'm storming through the woods.

I can hear her behind me, so naturally I start running. There's literally no way she can outrun me. I mean, I play striker on the soccer team, so good luck you purple-haired....She grabs my arm because somehow her little legs are really fast too, and I feel like my arm is being pulled out of its socket, and then there goes Pluto, running past both of us as fast as she can, her leash trailing behind her on the ground. Mia and I stop and look at each other, and I realize how much my grandparents love that dog, and how I would hate to disappoint them if she ran away. None of this has been their fault. I take off after Pluto, the magical escape artist. Where is this dog going?

Let me tell you, this puffy rat-dog can run. I'm out of breath, sprinting uphill, and I'm losing sight of her. The sound of waterfalls fills my ears again, and I start to wonder what Pluto is even chasing. I hear Mia shouting "Estrellita!" at the top of her lungs, and then I see it. A waterfall. It isn't one that we toured. It's racing down from a large rock wall, surrounded by tall trees and spilling into a river. I see the tail end of Pluto's leash disappear into a small cave behind the waterfall and I'm imagining a bear or a lion or whatever lives in Michigan caves just waiting to enjoy a caramel colored puffy snack. I'm still racing up the pathway and I can tell it narrows in front of me to hug the wall and eventually widen behind the falls. Mia sprints past me and darts into the cave. She's pretty much soaked now because the waterfall sprays all over her, and I know my turn is next. I almost stop myself because I'm wearing my favorite red flannel, a nice pair of Levi's and my black Vans and I don't feel like getting my clothes wet. But I realize that Mia, as scrappy as she is, isn't going to be able to fight off a bear all by herself, and so I follow her.

At first it's really dark, so I'm following the sound of Pluto's annoying bark, and Mia's voice, but it's hard to hear either because the waterfall is echoing through the cave. My eyes are having a hard time adjusting. I almost slip and fall but I catch myself. Then I hear shouting, and it's not Mia's voice. In fact, it's not just one voice; it's multiple voices. It's a lot of shouting, and I suddenly wish I was running in the opposite direction. My heart starts to beat really quickly and I'm not sure if it's because I'm so out of breath or if I'm freaked out. I can't turn around, though, because Pluto is up there, and so is Mia. As annoying as she is, the last thing I want is for something bad to happen to her, so I run faster and faster. Suddenly light is blinding me as I reach the end of the cave.

So, I'm realizing it wasn't a cave, but it was some kind of tunnel. And now I'm also soaking wet because I apparently ran through another waterfall. My jaw literally hits the ground as I see arrows flying above me and hitting an extremely tall tree to my left. I hear the clang of swords clashing together and shields ramming each other and more voices shouting and screaming at each other. Men and women are locked in an intense battle. There's lots of people with large swords and axes and shields. I'm starting to back up in fear and confusion, and I'm wondering if I've stumbled into some weird civil war reenact-ment or something. Then I wonder if Michigan was part of the Civil War or not and I'm regretting my decision to not really pay attention during World Geography, and then I'm wondering if we studied wars in World Geography. I'm terrified and I have to go to the bathroom. This is really realistic and I notice that some are wearing green and others are wearing orange. Then a dude dies in front of me, and this just got REAL. Then I see a scary dude holding a green banner with a tree stitched into the fabric, and an orange banner with a sun is even closer to me, and speaking of suns, I look up and I'm pretty sure there are two of them in the sky. Then I'm wondering if there was something weird in that suspicious pot of beans Grandma cooked over the fire.

Mia is standing next to me, and I don't even remember cat-ching up to her. We look at each other and I swear we're making the same confused and freaked out face. Pluto suddenly jumps into my arms and she's shaking in fear and she's soaking wet.

I swallow because what I really want to do is throw up.

I look at the rat-dog. "Pluto, I have a feeling we're not in Michigan anymore."

Chapter 3
Study Questions

1. Why do you think Oliver avoids deep conversations?

2. Oliver has conflict with both Mia and his mom. What do you do when you have anger? How could Oliver apply the wisdom from James 3:9-10 to his life? How could you?

3. Oliver has an interesting conversation with his grandfather about what kind of man he wants to be. What do you think about his response? Do you believe him?

4. Read James 2:14. How does this connect with Oliver's conversation with his grandfather? How does it connect with your life?

5. If you find your actions don't match up with the faith you claim to have, what can you do? How can you stop doing things you don't want to do, and do the things you know in your heart you should?

Chapter 4:
So, I Look for a Faun
Mia

I am so confused, and also freaking out. As I stumble through the second waterfall, I spot a group of people that stop me dead in my tracks. They are wearing kind of medieval-ish clothing, but not suits of armor, more like Robin Hood type of clothing, but not funny looking tights, more like leather and boots and green. And they are fighting the people in orange, who are dressed in tunics, cloth gauntlets, tan pants, and boots.

LARPers, I decide.

But the fighting looks too real. Scratch that. The fighting is real. "Psycho LARPers!" I shout at Oliver, who is rooted to the spot where he's standing with a damp Estrellita in his arms. I grab Oliver's arm, like I did a few minutes ago when I was super angry at him. I'm still angry at him, but I'm mostly just terrified at this point. He snaps out of his shock as we begin to run back into the waterfall. We have to warn Mami, Lito, and Lita, probably the park rangers too, and get as far away from here as possible.

I'm just stepping into the pooled water when Oliver's arm gets ripped out of my hand. I see him yanked away by a woman in green. Estrellita yelps and falls to the ground, darting behind a bush. I turn around to run after Oliver, but instead I smash into another green soldier. This guy is young, maybe still in high school, and he has a creepy scar across his cheek and nose, a sharp contrast to his light skin.

He grabs my shoulders. "You're coming with me."

Oh, I most certainly am not.

Overcome with panic, I kick him in the shins, and I'm so glad I chose to wear my black combat boots today. He grunts and loses his balance, but he doesn't let go of me and we both topple to the ground.

The soldier sits up first. I try to roll away, but he grabs my sweatshirt and raises a fist. "Sorry about this," he says, while not sounding at all sorry, and I see his fist coming right toward my face.

But then he screams and is flung to the side by an arrow that has struck his arm. I scramble to my feet to see Oliver's attacker fall to the ground beside him. She doesn't get up again, but mine is able to stumble away into the thick forest. I see the archer come into view, a tall Black man dressed in orange. He draws his sword, a real-life sword, and pursues the soldier that got away.

Oliver rushes over to me. His clothing is wet and rumpled, but he looks okay.

"What is going on?!" I scream.

"We have to get out of here!" he yells back.

There are a bunch of green soldiers closing in on us. The orange archer swordsman guy reappears. "Get behind the tree," he directs us. He points to a large oak-like tree that is the opposite direction from the waterfall.

I don't know who he thinks he is that we should listen to him, but he did just save both our lives, and he has a sword and we don't.

We get behind the tree.

"Am I dreaming?" Oliver whispers as an arrow whizzes by.

I don't answer, because I'm not sure, but I do close my eyes and cover my ears with my hands. I am like this for a while. My only source of comfort is Oliver's leg brushing up against mine, reminding me I'm not alone.

Which is something I'll never admit to him.

Eventually, the guy who saved us comes around our side of the tree and says, "Are you alright? It's over now."

"Who the heck are you people?!" I shout, trying to ignore the unmoving green soldiers scattered on the ground. A handful of orange soldiers have been lost too, but I see that the majority of them are still okay, if not a bit injured here and there.

"There's no time to explain," a girl says as she approaches.

While she is dressed the same as the other soldiers, a gold band circles her head. I see the rest of the soldiers stand at attention. A girl is in charge? I'm listening.

"I am honored to make your acquaintance," she continues. "I am Princess Evora of the Desert Kingdom of Rukin."

"The what now?" I ask.

"Please don't interrupt me, Ambassador," Princess Evora says. I raise an eyebrow.

If I were to categorize her, I'd say she's the typical popular girl in any given high school. Very Western standard of beauty: thin, tall, pinned up blonde hair. "We are from Rukin. We came to find you." She says this looking at Oliver. I look at him, too, and realize he's gone all googly-eyed for the "Princess." Great. Useless.

"To find *him?*"

"Both of you, I suppose. But, as I said, we don't have time. I promise, I can explain more once we get to safety."

She turns to leave, but I step in front of her. "Hold on. You said we're in Rukin? I've never heard of Rukin, Michigan. We're not going anywhere with you until you tell us what's going on with…" I gesture to all the dead soldiers on the ground, feeling nauseous, "this."

The princess sighs and holds the bridge of her nose. "Let me start over and try to make this simple to understand: I am Princess Evora. This is part of my army. We came here to find you, the Ambassadors. I don't know what you mean by 'Mitch-again,' but you are in Elior now. There are seven kingdoms, and you happened to come through the portal in one of the bad ones. We are in the Forest Kingdom of Canterbor. The people we were fighting were trying to stop you. Kill you. They would have if we hadn't intervened. Now, as we are still in enemy territory, I implore you, please come with us. Every moment we spend here makes it more likely that more Canterbor soldiers will find you. I can answer all your questions once we reach safety."

"What do you mean by 'Ambassadors'?" Oliver asks suspiciously. Oh, good, his mind is back from vacation.

"And why does Canterbor want to kill us?" I add.

"And what is 'Elior'?" Oliver questions.

"And what portal are you talking about?"

I don't think Princess Evora anticipated how many questions we would have.

And then I think of every land or distant world I've read about or watched in movies and my recent experience in the waterfall cave. It couldn't be. Could it?

"Is Narnia real?" I whisper to Oliver.

Oliver whispers back, "She said we're in Elior, though? Or Canterbor? Or both?"

"Where are the fauns in scarves?" I look at the tall guy next to me. "Do you serve the evil ice queen?"

"I serve Princess Evora of the Desert Kingdom of Rukin," he says confusedly. His voice is deep and his face is kind. I decide I like him. Plus, he saved our lives, so there's that.

"We will have time for pleasantries later," Princess Evora says, making eye contact with Oliver. "Please let us take you to safety."

"Okay," I agree.

"Seriously?" Oliver exclaims.

"I don't know about you, but nobody's ever tried to kill me before. These people kept us alive. I'm going with them."

Then, one of the soldiers bursts out of the foliage with Estrellita in her arms, licking her face. "Is this yours?" the woman asks, laughing.

She hands her over to me. "Thanks."

"My name is Lucius," the life-saver guy says. "I am Princess Evora's personal bodyguard."

"Mia."

"And yours?" The princess asks Oliver.

"Oliver," he gulps. Useless.

"Oliver," she smiles. "Come with me?" She extends her hand. After a moment of hesitation, he accepts.

Princess Evora directs an elite team of scouts to stay behind and look out for anyone trailing us. Then she sticks us on horses, something I've never desired to experience, and we're riding out ahead of the main forces, along with Lucius and three other tough looking soldiers.

A few minutes later I hear a sound like thunder. "What was that?" Oliver asks.

"Looks like rain," Evora notes. "Hopefully we can find shelter before it hits."

It doesn't look like rain to me, but maybe it looks different in this land beyond the waterfall?

"What does your shirt mean?" Lucius asks me.

I glance down at my wet, black sweatshirt that says "Friends, Not Food" in big white letters with a cow with big, sad eyes underneath.

"It means that animals have rights, too," I say self-consciously.

"The legends are right," he nods. "The Ambassadors are good people. They can save us all."

"We still need to address that," I mention. But I think I'm okay going with them. These weird people in this weird place seem to know something about us that we don't. And who would I be if I just turned around and went back through the waterfall now? Who knows what kind of story I'd miss out on?

Chapter 4
Study Questions

1. What evidence is there that Mia still cares about Oliver, even though she pretends not to? Why does she do this?

2. Have you ever been in a new situation? How did you get to know new people and surroundings?

3. Read 1 Peter 2:11-17. How could Mia and Oliver apply those verses to their situation?

4. Read 1 Peter 2:9. Have you ever been chosen for something? What did that feel like? How did you know God was choosing you?

Chapter 5:
So, I Don't Have Service Here
Oliver

Horses are awful. And mean. I don't know why all these animals hate me, but the feeling is definitely mutual. Let's call him "Horse," because I refuse to give him a creative name, but Horse is especially boney and uncomfortable. Let's get this straight: I'm a city boy, and Horse knows this. I'm pretty sure it's why he decides to run off from the others randomly, and why he stinks so bad, and why he's constantly, um, how should I put this? Visiting the little boy's room? Yeah. Disgusting. Meanwhile, Mia's animal is behaving wonderfully, oh yeah, and she gets to ride with Lucius, who appears to have been (driving?) horses his entire life. Me? I get my own terrible black spotted creature.

So, let's talk about Princess Evora. Okay, it's not like I could call Courtney anyway, believe me, I've been trying, but my phone is definitely not working up here in Elior, Michigan. Yeah, they say we're in Elior, that we're in the Forest Kingdom of Canterbor, but how is this possible? Except, I can't help but look at that second sun in the sky and wonder what kind of movie set I've stumbled across. I want to talk to their special effects person because all of the death and makeup effects are way too realistic and I really must be dreaming, but back to Evora. She keeps looking back at me from her horse, and I smile at her, and she smiles back. And then I remember watching her fight and thinking that I better not make her mad because she could definitely cause damage. I want to say something charming but I don't want to look stupid, so I don't say anything except smile awkwardly, and eventually she stops looking back at me. Horse starts making weird noises, and it's trying to run off into the woods again, so two of the soldiers with us are pulling on Horse's reins and now we're stopping for water.

I put my phone into airplane mode because I don't have my charger with me, and I'm wondering if I'll be able to find an outlet in the middle of the woods. This is doubtful. I slip my phone back in my pocket. Where are we, really? This is so bizarre. Last I checked it was June, but these woods are looking more and more like Texas in November: brown, dead, and ugly. Princess Evora, Lucius, and the other four soldiers are taking care of watering their ugly pets and are busy talking to each other in hushed tones. Meanwhile, Mia is sitting on a log, scribbling something in her dumb journal. I mean, really Mia, is now the time?

"Hey, I think we should make a run for it," I suggest, sitting beside her.

"And go where?" she asks without looking up.

"Um, back to the campsite, through that waterfall cave thing."

"And when we're attacked by the evil forest soldiers, are you planning on fighting them off?"

I sit up straighter. "If I have to," I say. Unfortunately my voice cracks at the same time. Hooray for puberty.

"Go for it," she mumbles. "We don't even know where we are."

"Have you noticed that second sun?" I mutter.

"Yeah."

"Last I checked, Earth only has one, right?"

"Right."

"You don't remember traveling through space with me, do you? To another planet?"

"No. Just Estrellita chasing a squirrel through a waterfall."

"Oh, was that what she was chasing?" I ask, looking at Pluto who has joined Horse at the little pond we've come across. I'm sure they're going to be great friends.

"Oliver, I'm a little busy at the moment, if you haven't noticed," she snips, still not looking at me. I want to grab her diary and throw it into the pond, but instead I walk away. As usual, Mia is totally unhelpful, and I'm actually missing that horrible tent and those nasty beans at the moment, and my wonderful, perfect headphones that I would do anything to have about now.

How can she be so chill about being here? This is literally insane. We've been rescued/captured by these crazy actors and a hot princess and I'm wondering if I've entered into some kind of video game.

"Is everything okay? You're looking a little unwell. Cerise, bring the boy something to eat please." Evora is now staring at me and I don't think I've ever seen such gorgeous brown eyes before. Usually I'm into blue or green eyes like mine, but there's something about her eyes that is captivating. Also, she referred to me as "boy" and I'm pretty sure we're like the same age. So, I decide to just ask.

"Um, how old are you?"

Cerise, a tall female soldier in an orange headband thing, is handing me a loaf of bread and I'm suddenly devouring it like it's a bag of Skittles or something.

"I am in my sixteenth year."

"Oh," I say with way too much bread in my mouth. I definitely must be dreaming, because now her hand is on my forehead, and her hand is so soft for being so lethal.

"You don't feel warm. I just assume all of this must be a little overwhelming for you. It's such a relief you've made it."

"Hey, glad to be here," I say, just deciding to go with it. This girl really is into this whole thing and I wonder how much they're paying her to prank us. Then I wonder who "they" are, and how they would be able to pull off the reality of a second sun. I just decide I'm dreaming; I must have hit my head in that cave back there, and I'm probably lying on the ground right now and Pluto is eating my shoelaces and I'm so dead asleep I can't even do anything about it. So, I'll play along until I wake up.

"Your arrival is more important than you may realize."

"What do you mean?" Mia asks as she walks up beside us. I can tell she's pretty impressed with Evora, but the princess can't seem to keep her eyes off of me. Maybe this dream is pretty lit after all.

"Don't you realize who you are?" she questions with wide eyes. Cerise and Lucius stop what they're doing and look at us.

"Oliver and Mia Miller?" I ask with a grin.

"Mia De la Cruz," Mia corrects. Of *course* she has to use Mom's maiden name. But Dad is still her dad, changing her name won't change that.

"You're the Ambassadors. Only you can seal the portal in the frozen gate."

"Can you please explain these portals?" Mia asks. Evora doesn't look at her.

"Can't we use that portal to take us home?" I question. I mean, I'm down to help these people with whatever, but closing a portal doesn't sound like we'd be going back home.

"Sit down. Let me try and explain."

Mia sits down on the ground, and I sit across from her, right next to Evora. What? Yes, I remember Courtney, there's nothing wrong with just *sitting* next to this girl, okay?

"Long ago a Dark Prince ruled Elior. His laws were unfair. He was selfish and cruel, and the people lived in fear and turmoil. Luckily, Zohar was able to lead a rebellion against him. The Dark Prince fell, and now Zohar rules the seven kingdoms of Elior as Emperor."

I'm pretty sure I've seen this movie, but I keep listening.

"What does this have to do with us?" Mia asks, looking totally confused.

"You aren't the first to come here from your world. Many have before, and they saw the cruelty of the prince."

"The Ambassadors," I state.

"Yes," she answers. "They helped Zohar with the rebellion. He would not have been able to defeat the prince without them. I wish this was the end of the story." She swallows uncomfortably. "The truth is, not all follow Zohar. There are two kingdoms that have risen up in open rebellion against him. They hope to return the Dark Prince to Elior."

Yikes. "Let me guess, the Forest Kingdom of Canterbor," I say. What? I have a good memory.

"Yes, and the Frozen Kingdom of Kaalinon."

"The forest soldiers would have killed you. I'm so glad we got to you first."

"But why?" Mia asks, as Pluto jumps into her arms. The dog glares at me. I glare back. It's her fault we're here.

"Because only you can seal the portal, and the followers of the Dark Prince will do whatever they can to stop you."

"But I thought he was dead." Now I'm swallowing uncomfortably. For a dream this is really quite detailed, and I'm wondering if I should steal Mia's diary to take some notes.

"It is said he waits behind the portal in the frozen gate. His followers are anxiously trying to bring him back to Elior. Only the Ambassadors can seal the portal." Her eyes meet mine. "Only *you* can." I gotta admit, it's hard to look away. But I do.

"So, let me get this straight, we have these forest and ice soldiers who are trying to keep this dark portal open so their evil prince can return to destroy your world?"

"His looming presence has already begun to eat away Elior. Don't you see his dark effects?"

I did notice how ugly the dying trees were. I also notice the grass is pretty dry and there isn't a flower to be seen.

Mia crosses her arms. "So how are we supposed to seal this portal?"

Evora suddenly looks up. "We've stayed too long. As long as we remain in the forests of Canterbor your lives are in danger. We must head north to the deserts of Rukin, my home. We can regroup there, and I can really give you all the information you need." She stands. "After you seal the portal to his dark realm, I can return you here, and you can go home." She sighs, and her beautiful face looks desperate. "Please help us," she asks. And let me tell you, it's really hard to deny someone so gorgeous.

And I find myself standing too. She easily mounts her horse, and I'm suddenly feeling like as long as I'm here I might as well do what I can to help her, or at least until I wake up.

Mia looks more confused than ever, and I decide it's a good look on her. My eyes search the trees and I'm happy now that we're with Lucius and these Desert Kingdom folk. They're gonna do whatever they can to keep us safe, and I'm gonna do whatever I can to find a charger.

Chapter 5
Study Questions

1. Explain Oliver's attitude and his outlook on life. How is this shown as he thinks about his situation and interacts with others?

2. Oliver struggles with selfishness. Where in this chapter do we find evidence of that? Do you struggle with selfishness? How can you find ways to focus more on others instead of yourself?

3. In an earlier chapter, Oliver told his grandfather that the most important thing to him was finding his true purpose and showing people God. Read 2 Peter 1:5-11. What light does this shed on the amount of faith Oliver has in his life?

4. Focus specifically on 2 Peter 1:9. Sometimes we are shortsighted to our struggles. Take a moment and uplift a prayer to God that He will show you your flaws and that He will take them away so you can be more like Him.

Chapter 6:
So, the Stars are the Same
Mia

I have been taking so many pictures. The thing about fantasy stories that take place in other lands (Which are maybe real? Who knows anymore?) is that those kids didn't have iPhones. I'm snapping everything I can find including the kind of grungy forest that reminds me of summer in Texas, one particularly tall tree, and Oliver's sour face when his horse tries to run him into said tree.

Luckily, I grabbed my backpack when I started chasing my brother through the forest, because it means I have it now. There's not a lot inside that I can use for an extended adventure, but there are some useful items like my journal, pen, Chapstick, mascara, a water bottle, and my antidepressants.

I had a couple really bad years after my dad left. Real dark and unpleasant stuff. I don't want to get into that.

Oh, and also I have my phone charger, which is useless out here but still funny because Oliver cares way more about reception than me.

I'm having a good time. It feels like this birthday party I had when I turned eight. I had some really good friends in San Antonio, where I used to live. There were six of us who had been together since kindergarten at this little Adventist school, and we did everything together. And they just liked me for me.

Anyway, I moved to Cedar Park, Texas after the divorce and I had a lot of trouble making friends. It was during those couple of years that I mentioned earlier, and by the time I had resurfaced from the haze of depression, it was the end of middle school and my reputation had been set.

So, in a way, I feel like I've kind of got a second chance here. Maybe things can be different now.

"So, how do we close this portal thingy?" Oliver asks as we sit down to eat another rushed meal. It's been a few days of us traveling, traveling, traveling, stopping a few minutes to eat, traveling again, and then sleeping. Since I didn't foresee to put a change of clothes in my small backpack, this means I've been stuck in the same t-shirt, sweatshirt, ripped jeans, and combat boots the whole time. Oliver, too. He seems very upset about his fancy shoes getting all dirty. Always with the name brands, that kid. Princess Evora promises that she'll hook us up with all kinds of stuff once we reach her palace, her real palace, in Rukin. And we're almost to the border. Dense, yet sickly looking foliage has given way to more and more sky, and the dirt is becoming sandier. We're almost to the Desert Kingdom.

"You'll need to be trained in Aveth," Princess Evora tells him. She looks regal even after traveling on horseback for so long. Is she, like, bathing when nobody's paying attention? When would she have the time?

I've heard her mention this word off and on the last few days, but with no real explanation as to what it is.

"And how are you so sure that we will be good at that?" I ask. I'm not good at a lot.

"Anyone who truly has faith and believes in what the Emperor stands for can have Aveth," she smiles. "You'll see. As Ambassadors, you will be naturals."

"And then we can go home." Oliver raises an eyebrow.

"Why are you in such a rush?" the princess asks with wide eyes. Oliver's eyes widen, too. Gag.

I like the idea of being an Ambassador, Elior's version of the chosen one. Lucius tells us that this world is connected to all kinds of other places, not just ours, but they are dangerous and that's why we need to close off this open frozen gate in Kaalinon. That's a lot of pressure. Am I worried I'll totally mess everything up? You bet. But I want so desperately to do it right and to be seen for more than the weird loud kid with the purple hair. Maybe this is how. Maybe I was meant for this.

Who knows?

The *thwack* of an arrow startles me out of my thoughts as it embeds itself into a tree to my right. And suddenly it's chaos again.

In a blur of green, the Canterbor soldiers attack, I guess making a last-ditch effort to catch us before we reach the safety of the border to Rukin. Lucius, Cerise, Princess Evora, and the others quickly draw their weapons and jump into the chaos. Oliver and I drop our lunches and cower by the horses with our dog. You know, just cool Ambassador things.

"Here we go again," Oliver shakes his head.

"What are our lives?" I wonder.

Oliver takes his phone out of his pocket for the hundredth time and checks for service.

I glare at him. "Some hero you are."

He glances up at me. No bars. Clearly. "I don't see you fighting the bad guys either."

"At least I'm not checking my phone."

"That's because you don't have a reason to check yours."

"Oh, yeah? What's yours?"

"None of your business!"

"Children, this is not the time!" Lucius calls in our direction from where he is locked in a swordfight with a Canterbor soldier.

We crouch lower behind another tree. "Ah, *tienes una novia, no?*"

"Stop doing that!" he shouts, turning red. "I know it's on purpose!"

"Then stop pretending you don't know what I'm saying!"

"You're not better than me, Mia, nobody thinks so!"

Impulsively, I grab his phone out of his hand and throw it into the woods. Oliver's mouth drops open. He is probably about to call me another name, but isn't able to because that kid with the scar on his face shows up again.

This time he goes for Oliver, who, despite his gangliness, tries to put up a fight. But the soldier has a sword and it's pointed at my brother who is still backed against the tree. I notice that his left arm is in a sling, and remember that he was shot in the last fight. I try to help Oliver, but the guy doesn't let me get any closer. "Come with me, and nobody gets hurt," he tells me.

I don't believe him for a second. But what am I supposed to do? I may be angry at Oliver, but I would never want him to get hurt. I raise up my hands to make it clear I wasn't gonna kick him in the shins again and take a step forward.

Evora darts over to us and shouts, "Stop!" which surprisingly stops the guy, and I sense some history there. These people know each other. "Let him go," she commands.

"You know I can't do that," the Canterbor soldier says with a clenched jaw. I'm beginning to think he's totally unhinged.

Lucius comes out of nowhere and hits the soldier on his injured arm. He grunts in pain and drops his sword to grab his arm. Evora kicks the sword away and Lucius raises his own for the killing blow. I close my eyes.

"Leave him," Evora commands.

I open my eyes. Everyone, including the Canterbor soldier, is looking at her with question mark faces.

Then, another Rukin soldier shouts for us to jump on the horses, so I grab Estrellita and do what she says, and we're fleeing from the Canterbor attackers before you can say "Turkish Delight."

We manage to outrun them somehow, and I notice that this time Evora and Lucius stay behind to ward them off. She must really be able to hold her own.

After a while, we make camp for the night. The princess still hasn't caught up with us, so we also plan on waiting here until she finds us. We're close to Rukin and should reach the border tomorrow.

Oliver and I don't speak.

That night, I find myself unable to sleep, even through the pure exhaustion that comes from running for my life. Sometimes I have insomnia, and I'm also angry, so I figure it's a combination of those things.

I push back the sleeping bag thing I was given on the first night and disturb Estrellita's sweet little dog snoring as I push her off of me. Grabbing my pen and journal, I settle down nearby with my back to a tree stump. The guy on watch nods at me. "Don't go too far."

The moonlight is just bright enough peeking through the thinning trees. I start to sketch a picture of a waterfall buried in a forest.

I add myself looking confused, then Estrellita barking at some animal, then Oliver looking dumb. My pen marks get darker as I draw his face and I take some creative liberty with unibrows, pointy ears and a pig tail.

I look up when I hear movement behind me. Princess Evora appears, golden hair spilling out of the pins in her hair. She looks less perfect and more rumpled than I've seen her before.

"You found us."

"Mind if I join you?" she asks politely.

"It's a free country," I shrug. Wait, is it, though? I mean, they have an Emperor...but they seem to like him. I realize Evora is confused by my statement. "You can sit down."

She tucks a strand of hair behind her ear. "Mia, I am sorry if we got off on the wrong foot. Sometimes I can be short with people, and I just...I often make terrible first impressions."

Okay, I'm intrigued. Maybe she's not Miss Popular after all. "I'm not good at first impressions either." Or sometimes second or third impressions.

"I just...I've worked so hard for this." She looks at me. "I have an older sister, Odynne, the Crown Princess. Everyone just seems to really like her. And then, there's me. Just...plain old me..."

Her voice trails off and we look at the stars together. I wonder if stars are the same in this world as in mine. It seems like the people are the same.

"I get it." I show her my Oliver-pig drawing.

She laughs softly. It's kind of a nice laugh. "You two don't seem very close," she remarks.

"We have nothing in common." I hear sadness in my voice, and it confuses me. "I guess I wish it was different." But there's too much baggage. Too many words and actions that can't be taken back.

"Well, you're both here," Evora remarks. "And, you know, I've never heard of more than one Ambassador coming through a portal at the same time. Maybe that means something. Or maybe only one of you was supposed to get through."

"I don't even know what being an Ambassador means."

"It means you're special, Mia," Evora smiles. "You're the hero we need to keep our kingdoms safe. And we start by closing that portal in Kaalinon."

"To stop the Dark Prince."

"Correct."

"What's so bad about him?"

Evora frowns and I quickly add, "Well, I wanna know why people are rebelling against the Emperor. If he's so great, then why the fighting?" I'm kind of into countercultural things myself. The whole idea of a rebellion would be intriguing if they weren't trying to kill us.

Evora sighs and looks at her hands. "This was long ago, but... when the Dark Prince ruled, the world was in turmoil. He was unjust. Selfish. Cruel. He reveled in striking terror in his people. The Emperor came to rescue us. I just wish everyone could see that." She looks so sad. She has so much faith.

48

I bite my lip. "So, we close the frozen gate in Kaalinon and that stops him from being able to return to the world. Assuming we don't get murdered by Canterbor first, right?"

"You're safe with me," she assures.

"What's your issue with that one guy?" My curiosity gets the best of me.

She seems taken aback, but answers anyway. "He has been trying to hurt me for a long time. This mission against you is just the latest. The Dark Prince's followers are relentless."

"I see. Sorry I brought it up," I say awkwardly.

"It's okay," she smiles sadly. "You know, I've never really had a friend before. Do you think we can be friends?"

"We'll see," I grin.

Evora nods and says that she is going to bed. I imagine she's pretty tired after fighting off the bad guys all day.

Left alone once again with my journal, I turn to a new page. At the top I write:

DARK PRINCE

Then, I add the words Evora told me.

The guy sounds pretty scary. I become determined to keep him from trying to take over Elior. I wonder if this really is my second chance. Maybe. Just maybe.

Chapter 6
Study Questions

1. Mia and Evora are jealous of their siblings. Are you jealous of anyone in your life? Read Hebrews 13:5,6. What do these verses tell you about jealousy?

2. Have you ever felt like you needed a second chance? Did you get it? How?

3. Read Hebrews 13:16,17. Why do you think Mia is interested in the rebellion? Is it ever okay to disagree with leaders?

4. If you found yourself in Mia and Oliver's situation, would you have confidence that you could be the hero? Why or why not?

Chapter 7:
So, Evora is a Flamethrower
Oliver

I remember this time when I lived in San Antonio before the divorce. I was around eight or nine, I think, and everyone was being picked for teams to play kickball. I haven't mentioned this about myself yet because it's kind of embarrassing, but I was really small when I was younger. I was shorter than everyone else and really thin, and kids called me *Chaparro*, which means "shorty." It was super annoying, and I think I learned in school somewhere that eating bananas and drinking milk would make me grow faster, so I ate and drank a ton of that, and to this day, every time I see a banana I want to barf. So anyway, there was this jerk in my class, Giovanni, and he was tall and pretty built for a 4th grader. He was always team captain or first picked. And this one day, I remember they were choosing players, and everyone kept getting picked, and then it was down to me and this girl with thick glasses. I remember Gio looking right at me, and whispering to the other guys, and then picking her over me. And I was crushed, and it pretty much always happened after that. Sometimes I'd just hide in the bathroom during recess. I remember going home that day and trying to tell Dad about it. He was working in his office at home.

"Hey, Dad?" I said.

"One second, Oli."

I remember waiting much longer than that, and then his phone rang, and he started talking to someone and he held up his finger to tell me to wait even longer. So I did, and I don't even remember how long I waited but it felt like forever, and because I was just a stupid kid I was holding back tears because I was embarrassed and I wanted to be like everyone else but I was just so short even Mia was taller and I hated it and I knew he couldn't do anything about it but I just wanted *someone* to talk to and Mom was baking with Mia.

Finally, he put the phone down and without even looking at me said, "What's up?"

"We played kickball today and…"

"Did you win?" he asked, still typing away on his laptop.

"Um, no, but they picked me last."

"Oh," he said. And that was *all* he said. His phone rang again, so I left and went to my room.

And I know he was really busy; I guess it wasn't a big deal, but after that, I never told him anything like that again. So, I decided after I moved to San Diego, I'd never let that happen to me in school. I joined soccer and tried really hard to be friends with the guys in my class.

I don't know why I'm thinking about this, except that I'm majorly depressed. Mia chucked my phone into the woods, and we had to flee after the attack, and Lucius literally threw me on the horse and we rode away, and they refused to let me go back for my phone. You never know how much you love something until it's gone, I guess. Farewell, sweet phone. I'm not talking to Mia and I don't plan to anytime soon.

It's gotten much hotter because we're in the Desert Kingdom of Rukin now. And it's what you'd expect: a lot of sand. If you think one sun blaring down on you is bad, try two. It's so hot my sweat is sweating, and they tell me we don't have much longer before we get to the palace. It's apparently in the middle of an oasis, and every time we are crossing a sand dune, I'm imagining the palace is almost within view, and then I'm disappointed by sand, sand, and more sand.

I take my shirt off and tie it around my head. What? Can I help if my giant muscles have Evora staring at me? I can't help it. Okay, they're not giant, but I have worked hard for what I have. Because I'm not talking to Mia right now, I feel the need to talk to *someone*, and I don't want to seem *too* into Evora, so I try really hard to get to know the other soldiers with us. I've gotten good at meeting new people, and even better at getting them to like me.

So, Cerise is really tall for a girl. She's super strong and she really likes arm wrestling. Yes, she beat me. But I put up a good fight. She's pretty cool, like she's a mom and everything. Then there's Linnetia who is twenty. She really likes Pluto and I'm not sure why. That rat-dog is super spoiled, she's pampered more than Princess Evora. Anyway, Linnetia has red hair and I can tell she can be pretty intense. Ralik is kind of lame, honestly. He's kinda weird, and reminds me of this kid back in San Diego, Dane. The teachers all made us sit around and talk about how the guys were "bullying" Dane, and how Dane was "different." They didn't explain to us what that even meant, but he talks kinda slow and won't stop moving. They'll let him pace back and forth in the classroom. He's honestly super weird and I stay away from him mostly, unless Rodrigo says something hilarious about him. It's hard not to laugh, you know? So yeah, Ralik is like that. He's cross-eyed, doesn't say much, but he sounds weird when he talks and he's kind of slower than the others.

Jai is my favorite. I think he's my age, but I always hear him and Linnetia cracking jokes about Ralik. It's just stupid stuff, but it's funny. They make him carry their gear sometimes or they'll ask him questions over and over again, and then laugh about his answers after he goes away. I'll laugh with them. The three of us get along pretty well. They all talk to me more than Mia. Mia just kinda writes in her diary.

So, I haven't woken up yet, and either this is the longest dream in the history of the world, or all of this is somehow real. I'm just going along with it. I guess I don't have much of a choice.

Lucius tells us we're maybe a day or two away, and we've stopped for a bit of a rest. I get off of Horse, happy for the break. Mia disappears with Pluto and her diary and Evora sends Jai and Linnetia off to look for some food, cactuses, or sand critters, I guess? (Gross.) Ralik is being useless as usual, and almost immediately takes a nap, while Cerise is training with Lucius. This leaves Evora and I on a blanket, and I'm honestly stoked to have some alone time.

We've had a bit of some scattered conversation here and there, but there's usually someone else around. Now's my chance, because honestly, I decide I wasn't super into Courtney anyway. I guess I'm just not really feeling it anymore with her. Besides, my relationship with Courtney was full of drama, and my relationship with Evora is chill.

"Tell me about your palace," I say, leaning back on my elbows and stretching out my legs. As much as I want to cut my Levi's into shorts because it's so hot, I just can't bear to destroy them.

I'm getting super tan, and I'm trying to flex my abs as much as possible. Yes, they're there, they are small, but they are there.

"You'll really like it," she breathes, taking a sip of water from her canteen. She has her hair up, and man she's gorgeous. "I don't know how it'll compare to the cities in your world."

"San Diego is perfect. Perfect weather. Nice beaches. Lots to do. Wish I could take you there sometime."

"I'd love to see it," she smiles. And I never want that smile to go away. "Do you miss it?" she asks.

I really haven't thought about it much. It's been so crazy. "Honestly, it's been fun meeting all of you," I say, with my best smile. "What about you? Do you miss your...palace?"

"It's been nice to be away," she says, looking into the sky. There isn't a cloud up there. Reminds me of San Diego skies. "It's not always...easy there."

"What do you mean?"

"My parents, they have a lot of expectations, mostly for Odynne."

"Odynne?"

"My older sister, the crown princess of Rukin, the next in line for the throne. Sometimes it's hard to get their attention."

I think of all the times I try to get Dad's attention, but he's always so busy, and now with Tracy and Zoey, there's a lot going on. "I know what you mean."

She looks at me. "Yeah, but I mean, *you're* an Ambassador. Don't you see how special you are?"

I scrunch up my face. "I mean, not really, I guess. I'm still confused about the whole Ambassador thing."

"When we introduce you to Aveth, and when you're able to use the power easily, hopefully it will start making sense."

"Hopefully."

"I want to please them, you know? I want to make them proud of me."

I get that. I don't say anything. I just put my hand on her wrist and squeeze a little.

"My dad is really close with Emperor Zohar, so this mission is really important to him. It's my chance to show him I can do just as much as Odynne. Plus, the Dark Prince must not return."

"What's the guy's deal?"

"When he ruled Elior, whenever people went against him or broke his laws, he would kill them. When Emperor Zohar came to power, he set us free."

"Sounds like it was rough."

"That's what they say. Emperor Zohar has been ruling for hundreds of years now. He's immortal."

"What?" I say, probably too loudly. "Like, he can't die?"

"He has Aveth; it grants eternal life."

"So, when I use Aveth, I'll have eternal life too?" I ask, completely confused.

She smiles. "Not exactly; it's difficult to explain."

Suddenly Jai and Linnetia are running in and Linnetia is screaming. Evora and I stand up, my heart is racing, and I don't even know why.

"Princess, we have a problem!" Jai shouts, and both of them are out of breath. Ralik wakes up, and Mia hurries over with Cerise and Lucius. They all look worried.

"What is it?" Evora asks.

"A Horn Terror!" Jai shouts.

"Heading this way!" Linnetia adds, and suddenly everyone has pulled out their weapons.

"What's a Horn Terror?" Mia calls out, but there apparently isn't time for explaining because everyone is running in its direction, except for Mia and I who are standing uselessly by the horses and Pluto.

"Ralik, keep them safe!" Evora instructs, and I'm honestly *not* feeling safe with the loser guard, and I'm wondering why he's even a soldier if he isn't like everyone else.

"What's a Horn Terror?" Mia asks Ralik, who is standing in front of us with his sword drawn, as the others disappear over a sand dune. We can hear shouting and grunting and growling and

Ralik swallows uncomfortably.

"You don't want to know," he mutters.

I want to see it and I'm tired of hiding behind horses and bushes and trees and losers so I grab an extra sword from Lucius's supply bag and I'm running up the sand dune.

"Are you crazy?" Mia shouts out, but I don't even turn around.

And maybe I am crazy, or maybe I'm just tired of sitting back and not being helpful or useful or good at anything in this world. I'm racing up the hill and I can't even begin to describe what I see but I'll do my best. First of all, it has giant teeth, like even bigger than Mia's. Oh, and two giant feet. They call it Horn Terror for a reason, I mean, the (guy?) has ten of them. He's black and scaly but he has fur and I think he's having a bad day because he's smashing against Jai's shield and Jai is strong, because he's holding his own. Mr. Horn Terror is really tall, and I think he's buff behind all those scales and fur. Now he's smashed Jai to the ground and he's about to stomp on him with his giant feet, but Cerise and Linnetia are shooting arrows which are literally doing nothing to him. Then he's charging at Evora and I'm running at him, swinging my sword like Link from Super Smash Brothers, but Lucius beats me to him and he literally slams the beast with his body. Like, Lucius is big, but not that big, and Horn Terror isn't very impressed, and he's about to swing a massive claw at him when suddenly Evora is sending fire bolts at it.

Wait, what?

Evora is shooting rays of fire at the monster, and Horn Terror is now on fire, and he's smoking and running away, and moaning, and maybe he's crying. I mean, I would be crying.

"How did you do that?" I shout at her.

"Aveth," Lucius calls out.

They're gonna teach me that? Awesome.

"We must leave," Evora says casually, like she didn't just act like a flamethrower. "Horn Terrors travel in packs. Let's go." Yikes.

Later that night, after most of the others are asleep, I'm having trouble shaking the events of the day from my head. Also, for some reason I can't stop thinking about Dad. Like, our relationship is fine, I've spent all these years with him. I left with him for San Diego. I'm cool with Tracy. I'm a good older brother to Zoey. Like, it's chill. But for some reason, the memory of that random day I tried to tell Dad I wasn't picked in kickball just won't go away. And the day I tried to show him a paper I wrote. And when I needed some advice about a girl. And that awesome soccer game when I actually scored. Dad wasn't there. He was somewhere with Tracy.

"Having trouble sleeping?" Lucius asks. He's so legit I want him to teach me how to fight.

"Yeah, kinda."

"Me too." And suddenly he's sitting next to me. "You were brave today. Charging a Horn Terror, while not the smartest thing, took courage."

I smile to myself. I've never thought of myself as brave before. I guess I never had to be. "Thanks. I want you to teach me how to fight. And I want Evora to teach me Aveth."

"When we get to the Desert Palace, and after I've seen Kessia and Vyn, I will make the time."

"Kessia and Vyn?"

"My wife and son," Lucius smiles and looks into the stars. "I miss them....*so...much.*"

And suddenly I wonder if Dad misses me, and I wonder what having a dad like Lucius would be like.

"Oliver," Lucius's big brown eyes are looking down at me, "we're really glad you're here. Looks like we have the makings of a *true hero.*" He smiles and places his big meaty hands on my back, then he walks away, and for a moment, not being picked all those years ago doesn't seem to matter anymore.

I've been chosen; I was picked first.

And I'm gonna make him proud.

Chapter 7
Study Questions

1. Have you ever been bullied? How did that feel?

2. Why does Oliver make fun of Dane and Ralik if he was bullied when he was younger?

3. How we treat each other is so important! Being different than others is okay, in fact, God created us all uniquely and so individually! What can we do to help include others who are left out? What if we are left out ourselves, where can we turn?

4. Read Hebrews 10:23-24. Now read Hebrews 11:1. What is faith? What if there is a connection between the faith that you have in God, and how you treat others? What would that look like?

Chapter 8:
So, Santa Tells Us About the Gate
Mia

Thank goodness we've made it to the Oasis in Rukin. We spent a pretty miserable time trekking through the desert. It is so very hot here. And I live in Texas, so when I say it's *hot*, I mean it's hot. It does get pretty chilly at night, though. I ditched my sweatshirt days ago, and only wear it to sleep. During the day I roll up the sleeves on my t-shirt, but I'm ready for that new set of clothes that was promised. Oliver, of course, has stopped worrying about wearing shirts altogether. Typical. He thinks he's so macho. I watch him now laughing with Jai, his new soldier buddy.

Oliver still isn't talking to me. Like, at all. And when I hear him and the soldiers snickering, I can't help but wonder if they're laughing at me.

The Oasis is beautiful. I was beginning to wonder how anyone could live in a Desert Kingdom, but now I get it. There are lots of rocky hills on the outer rim, with a lake in the center. The houses and buildings and stuff are all wedged in between the hills and the lake, and there are a whole lot of palm trees and cacti. But, even here, I feel the suns beating down on me. I don't sunburn easily, but I could do with some eco-friendly sunscreen. My brother, who seems to believe he's super tan, is turning pretty red like Bob the Tomato.

"There it is," Evora catches my attention. "My home."

I turn to see a palace that is the same khaki type of color as the surrounding hills, so much so that I didn't even see it at first. It climbs one of the hills, with rectangular towers and balconies sticking out here and there. It's actually very beautiful. I see Rukin's insignia, an orange sun, all over the place.

"Good because I am ready for a bath," I grin.

But the bath has to wait for a little bit since the princess has returned and everyone seems very excited about that. People keep coming up to her and bowing. If I thought she was lying before, I have no doubt she is who she says she is now. Pretty soon, an escort shows up to take us to the palace in a couple large carriages.

Oh, and the carriage is pulled by straight up UNICORNS! "This place rocks," I whisper to my new friend, the unicorn, as I pet him.

"Do you not have the same creatures in your world?" Lucius asks me. The others are talking with the palace escort and loading up all our stuff.

"Not unicorns!" I exclaim, a bit too loudly. "Look, this guy's horn is the same color as my hair!" I show him.

"They come in all kinds of colors," he chuckles.

"We don't have the...what are they...the Horn Terrors or whatever either." I can still picture Oliver running stupidly toward it with a sword as if he thought he was actually gonna defeat it. The Horn Terror seemed more scared of Estrellita, who bravely barked at it.

"Count yourself lucky, then," Lucius tells me. "Many of those dangerous beasts roam the desert."

"And they just attack all the time?" The beast was scary and all, but I don't like seeing animals hurt (remember, the friends not food hoodie) and something in its eyes seemed off to me. I can't quite put my finger on it.

"It's their nature," he shrugs.

"Ow!"

I turn to see Oliver holding his finger where he sliced it on the sword he was allowed to keep after the animal incident. Seriously, whose idea was it to let him be around sharp objects?

Pretty soon, I find myself squished in a carriage, sandwiched between Ralik and Cerise with Estrellita on my lap. Across from me, Oliver sits with Jai.

I keep trying to catch Oliver's eye. I'm feeling a little bit guilty, okay? I didn't know Oliver wouldn't be able to get his phone before we left. But he still is pretending like I don't exist.

"Hey, Ralik," Jai breaks the silence. "What are you gonna do now that you're home?"

Ralik doesn't answer, as he looks out the window. His mind is somewhere else.

"Ralik, I'm talking to you." Jai kicks him with his boot.

Ralik jumps. "What?"

"What are you gonna do now that you're home?"

I don't like the smirk on Jai's face. Or Oliver's for that matter.

"I think I'll go feed my goats. They're my favorite."

Then, Oliver does something that boils my blood. He repeats what Ralik said in the same tone of voice while crossing his eyes and tilting his head. Jai bursts out laughing.

Ralik looks sadly out the window again.

"Shut up, Oliver," I snap.

"See what I'm saying?" Oliver mumbles to Jai, but loud enough for me to hear.

Jai laughs. "Hey, Ralik, I think Mia has a crush on you."

Ralik, if he hears Jai, chooses to not answer.

"Why don't you big jerks leave him alone?"

This isn't the first time Oliver has made fun of me. Neither of us were exactly popular in school, but back when we were at school together, Oliver would sometimes throw me under the bus (not literally) and make fun of me before the others had a chance to make fun of him. I know what he's doing. I can see right through him. He can be so shallow.

Jai and Oliver start whispering to themselves, grinning. I nudge Ralik. "Hey, don't listen to them. Estrellita has more brains than both of them combined."

Ralik doesn't answer but he nods his head.

"Do you like being a soldier?" I realize I've never talked to him before. I'm so awkward that I haven't really gotten to know anyone except for Lucius and Evora a little.

"I like my goats," Ralik tells me.

"Ralik's father purchased his place in the military," Cerise says as she leans over to me. "It's a very prestigious position. Looks good for the family."

"But he doesn't want to do it."

Cerise shrugs. "It's more common than you'd think."

I guess no world is perfect. At least in my world there's less of a chance of being mauled by a wild beast. Even so, I'm still pretty sure I'd rather stay here. Maybe I'll stay even after we close the portal. I think back to what Evora said about two Ambassadors from one place. I could be crazy, but making fun of someone who is different doesn't sound like the quality of a true Ambassador. Maybe I was the only one who was supposed to end up here.

We reach the palace itself, and already Rukin feels safer than Canterbor. There's something to be said about not fearing for your life all day.

As we step out of the carriage, I sneak another pat to Mia 2, the unicorn with the purple horn (see, Oliver, I can name things too). Evora's family stands waiting for us on the steps. She runs up to them and warmly hugs her father. I feel a sting of longing. Did Dad ever hug me like that? Not since he started building his new family. I miss Mami.

Evora turns to present us. "Father, this is Ambassador Mia and Ambassador Oliver." We step forward and awkwardly bow. I suddenly wish Evora had briefed us on Rukin's royal protocol.

"Two Ambassadors. This is nearly unheard of," the king remarks. "But I am glad to make your acquaintances. I am King Jethil. Emperor Zohar sends you warm greetings."

"They're very close," Lucius whispers to me.

"My daughter has told us much about you."

"Do you have telepathy on top of firebending?" I say as my mouth drops open.

Everyone looks at me, totally confused. Nobody gets my references. That's fine.

King Jethil is a rounded man, no angular features about him. He's got a reddish face and white beard, giving off super intense Santa Claus vibes. We are also introduced to Queen Valia, an older version of Evora, and Crown Princess Odynne, who I immediately dislike. Her hair is a little darker than Evora's, but they are clearly related.

Oliver and I are given a suite where we can clean up and the promise of meeting the royal family for dinner tonight.

"I can't get my own room even in a palace," Oliver complains to himself.

"This isn't a dream come true for me either," I sigh.

He huffs and follows the palace guard to our suite.

I'm not sure how, but there's some Eliorian version of A/C running so it's ridiculously cool and comfortable inside. The suite is some strange type of sand-colored stone, cool to the touch. Bright colors accent the brown walls. There is a purple couch, two separate rooms with a blue bed and a green bed, and orange rugs and curtains. I know it sounds like those colors would clash, but they actually look great, and I'm totally into it. Also, I am thrilled to discover running water in the bathroom! Okay, these people are more advanced than their horses and chariots would lead you to believe.

"You can bathe first," I tell Oliver, in a gesture of kindness. I know, I know, he's a jerk and he made fun of me like fifteen minutes ago, but deep down I always kind of believe the mean stuff he says, and also I lost his phone.

Instead of answering, Oliver plops down on the window seat, opens the window, and refuses to look at me.

"Okay, fine," I throw up my hands. "You can bathe in my dirty water." Which isn't exactly true, but I hope he thinks it is.

And, just like that, I am a new person. The water washes away the caked on sweat and dirt from our stressful journey north. I wash my hair and the water turns a little purple as some of the dye washes out. I somewhat sadly trash my jeans, t-shirt, and sweatshirt that have seen better days, in favor of flowy white pants and a salmon colored tunic-thing. I keep my combat boots, though. You never know when you'll need to kick somebody.

Oliver shoulders past me into the bathroom. I sink into the fluffy blue bed and proceed to draw a picture of Pig-Oliver with his stupid little sword and his stupid little shirtless self. Oliver appears a little while later dressed in similar white pants, but his shirt is green.

"Ready to go downstairs?" I venture. It's about dinner time.

Oliver glares at me, but at least he's acknowledging my existence. That's a step in the right direction.

"You're being really dramatic. It was just a cell phone. You can get a new one. All your stuff is backed up."

"I haven't had service in days!"

"Then it's just a camera!"

"How would you feel if I broke your phone right now?" Oliver snaps.

"Be my guest!"

Oliver has crazy eyes. Good luck finding my phone; it's in my backpack.

But he takes a couple long steps with his gangly legs, rips my journal from my hands and tosses it out the open window.

"No!" I jump off the bed, and without thinking, I slap him in the face. His cheeks are already red from the sun, but I see a new red mark begin to form immediately. Oliver just stands there fuming.

"Ahem." We look over to find a palace servant standing like a deer in the headlights in the doorway. "I'm here to take you to dinner."

Oliver slowly straightens his tunic and leaves the room. I rush to the window and look down, but we are kind of high up, and my blue journal is nowhere to be found. I hold back my tears. The royal family of Rukin won't see me cry. My stupid brother won't see me cry either. I won't give him that satisfaction.

I sit in stony silence at the dinner table. It's long and decorated all fancy. I turn away the mysterious but tasty-smelling meat in favor of the equally mysterious items without faces. Everything smells delicious, but tastes like sand in my mouth. My mind is whirling with all the lost notes in my journal. My therapist told me to start keeping it during the scary days, and there are private thoughts in there that nobody, not even Mami, has ever seen.

I'm pulled out of my thoughts by King Jethil as he clears his throat. "Princess Evora tells me you have not been completely informed as to your mission as Ambassadors. Is this correct?"

"We could use some guidelines," Oliver says. His left cheek is redder than the right one, and only I know why. That pang of guilt comes back, but I push it away. He's probably not even a real Ambassador; it was probably supposed to be just me.

He stands. "Long ago, when Elior was created, one portal appeared in six of the seven kingdoms, all except for the High Kingdom of Aresmond. The Ambassadors were used for years to oppress Elior's people, until the Emperor took charge and cast out the Dark Prince. Since then, the Ambassadors from other lands have aided Emperor Zohar in his quest to keep peace and beauty in Elior. All except for the Ambassadors from Kaalinon."

"The ice kingdom or whatever, where we're going," I clarify.

"Correct," he nods. "You must prevent the Dark Prince from reentering our land through that portal."

Evora adds, "As Ambassadors, your duty is to close the frozen gate in Kaalinon. We will find it in a cave in the snowy mountains."

"How do we close it?" Oliver asks.

"My daughter is a master in the use of Aveth. She will train you."

"You must use Aveth to close the portal," she says.

"It's just, like, a fighting tactic?" I wonder.

"It's so much more than that," Princess Evora smiles. "It has to do with faith as well. It has to do with the state of your heart." She touches Oliver's chest and I cringe.

"Now," King Jethil continues, "Kaalinon is one of the two openly rebellious kingdoms. The other is Canterbor, of course. This means that the open portal will be heavily guarded by Kaalinon soldiers. You will likely face a skirmish at the border, and then a full-on battle for access to the portal."

Battles? Fighting? I didn't sign up for this. The feeling of inadequacy creeps up my spine. I could barely handle the fighting that happened when we first came through the portal.

"Once you close the portal using Aveth, we will leave our troops there to ensure it is never opened again."

I raise my hand like I have a question for my English teacher. "If we use Aveth to close the portal, how is it able to be opened again?"

All four of the royal family look down sadly. "The followers of the Dark Prince have a counterfeit version of Aveth," Evora explains in a low voice. "It is blasphemous. And frightening. And they must be stopped."

"I see," I awkwardly mumble. Sorry I asked.

After dinner, I get permission to walk the palace grounds. The night air is cool now, so I fold my arms around myself. I try to locate my room window and search the ground in vain for my journal. About an hour later, I feel disappointment in my gut, and I'm close to giving up. I sit cross-legged on the cold stone, leaning my elbows on my knees. I stare at the bustling city across the lake.

I hear bugs that could be crickets making noise around me, and I watch the stars, those same stars, in the clear, open sky. I think of Oliver's eyes. I know it sounds weird, but something was nagging at me ever since I saw the flash of anger in his green eyes right before he threw my journal out the window.

I'm reminded of the Horn Terror that attacked us. It had that same look. That cornered look. "I'm still missing something," I murmur to myself. "What could I be missing?"

Out of seemingly nowhere, a man's voice comes from my left, and it's attached to someone casually strolling around the corner of the wall.

"Ba dum dee dum dee dum dee dai, ba dum dee dum dee dum dee dai..."

It's a strange old looking man with only one eye and a scraggly beard. He's wearing a coat and rags and twirling a stick between his fingers.

"Hello," I say suspiciously.

"Ba dum dee dum dee dum dee dand,
Beware the Blight, it scars the land,
Ba dum de dum dee dum dee dart,

Beware the Blight, it scars the heart…"

"I'm sorry, what's the Blight?"

He stops in front of me and his one eye stares into my soul. The guy just keeps on singing.

"The flame will burn and break and kill,
It blinds our eyes with fiery skill…"

I stand up hastily. "Once again, dude, are you trying to talk to me, or is this a folk song, or what's happening? I'm not…from around here…"

"But Ruach forgives, and pays the cost,
The true king returns that which was lost…"

"Sorry, I'm not getting any of this…" My voice trails off as the old man reaches into his coat and pulls out my blue journal. He hands it to me, bowing graciously, as he saunters off in the other direction.

"Ba dum dee dum dee dum dee dai, ba dum dee dum dee dum dee dai…"

I feel a chill that's not from the cool night air, but somehow seems familiar. I clutch my journal and run back inside the palace.

Chapter 8
Study Questions

1. Imagine how Mia and Oliver felt finally entering the palace in Rukin. How would you feel if you were in their situation?

2. Have you ever been chosen for something that you are nervous about? Read 1 Peter 5:6-7. How could this help you (or Mia) feel more confident about being chosen?

3. Mia gets mad at Oliver for throwing her journal out the window. Why would Oliver have done that? Why did Mia get so upset?

4. What do you think the old man's song meant? Read Hebrews 8:12 and say a prayer asking God to help you remember this promise.

Chapter 9:
So, Aveth is Hard
Oliver

"Again," Evora commands, as we stand in the square staring at each other. I'm still not entirely sure what I'm doing, but I'm really good at pretending to know. Basically I'm standing here, feet shoulder-width apart, arms up in the air, knees bent, like I'm some circus performer, and somehow, Aveth is supposed to shoot out of my hands and into the air if my "heart is right" and my "faith in the Emperor is enough." And this isn't like in school when the teacher asks you to pray, and you give the best prayer the class has ever heard, and you crack your eye open and you see your teacher nodding in approval. No. It's nothing like that. I'm not gonna lie, when she was explaining what I should be thinking about when trying to use Aveth I was really distracted by Evora's gorgeous face and I didn't pay very close attention, but I nodded enthusiastically like I did in Algebra 1. But I'm starting to realize I may not be able to fake my way through this.

"Oliver, you *have* to focus." Evora stares at me, and I realize I missed what she said again, but boy she looks prettier than ever. "Do you want to take a break?"

I look up at the balcony and notice King Jethil staring intensely down on me, and I'm reminded that I'm their greatest hope to stop the Dark Prince from returning, because clearly everyone knows that Mia is worthless. "Absolutely not. I'm ready. Again," I say dramatically like I'm Captain America.

"Remember, Aveth comes from within. It's already a part of you. The strength lives within you. Look deeply inside of your heart."

So, I close my eyes and pretend to look inside my heart, because honestly I'm not even sure what that means, and I'm lifting my arms above my head and I'm imagining fire bolts

71

shooting out of my fingers, but instead I start to yawn, because I actually have been doing this for a long time today.

"Am I boring you?" she asks a little bit intensely, and I open my eyes quickly and try to recover, but I can tell she's kind of upset.

"What? No! Come on, I just...I didn't sleep too well last night, and..."

"We can take a break." She steps back and moves to a sand-colored bench, sitting down on it. I take a quick glance up, and I notice King Jethil has returned inside. Man, Oliver, you really messed this up.

"Hey, we can keep going," I persist, but she's looking away now, leafing through some book she pulled out of somewhere.

"No, I think I pushed you too hard. I don't know why I thought this would be easy." And I can tell she's frustrated, and it's looking like she's more upset with herself than with me.

"Hey, I'm sorry I'm not a natural." I soften my tone. I really don't want her to be upset.

"No, it's okay. There's just a lot of pressure." And now she's looking up in her dad's direction, but it won't matter. He's gone. But her older sister, Odynne, stands there looking down on us and Evora sits up straighter. I can feel the tension, and it's clear Evora's wishing I was absolutely shooting fireballs into the air, and that she had been the one to teach me how. I'm feeling pretty worthless at the moment.

"I'll get it. I promise. It takes me a bit to get stuff someti-mes, but once I do, I'm unstoppable," I smirk.

And she tries to smile back but I can tell it's forced. "I have some things to attend to," she says, standing.

I'm not sure how to make things better, but I really want to. And I wish I could say something that would fix everything, that would immediately transform me into the hero I know they need, the hero I know I can be, but nothing comes to mind, so I'm standing too, watching Evora walk away, and now she's gone and I'm annoyed with myself for saying no-thing, and it's weird because I notice Odynne is also gone and suddenly I'm alone in the training square.

I'm feeling very sad at the moment, and kind of embarrassed, like that one game last year when it came to penalty kicks, and I lost us the game.

"Would you like some water?"

I turn, and there's the Crown Princess Odynne handing me a glass of water. She sure got down from that balcony quickly. So, I nod and take the glass, and I'm trying to be polite, but I'm totally on team Evora, so I don't want to be too nice.

"It's a mystery even I don't understand."

"Huh?" I ask.

"Aveth. I've never used it, but I've watched Evora train others in it."

"You don't use it?" I thought for sure the next in line to the throne would have this superpower. Evora should totally rule next.

"I don't. I realize how special it is, but," she looks down and away and I can tell she's struggling to figure out what to say, "it kind of terrifies me."

This surprises me, but I keep my chill. "Why?" I ask casually.

She looks around, like she's seeing if anyone is listening to our conversation, but I don't look away. Her face is the same shape as her younger sister's, but her hair is shorter and she's less pretty. She's taller and her nose is kinda pointy too. Points off for a pointy nose.

I guess we fear what we don't understand." Our eyes meet and her eyes are darker than Evora's. "All I can say is, don't give up. I've learned that strength comes to us when we least expect it to, and when we need it most."

And I'm wondering why Evora doesn't really like her sister who seems actually really nice to me, and for a moment, I get really nervous about heading to the ice kingdom to fight battles that I feel are totally unwinnable. It's like playing against Real Madrid and my leg is broken too.

She looks at me and smiles. "You can't have faith in someone you don't know." She breathes, and I nod, acting like I totally know what she's talking about.

"Thanks for the advice, but Evora's a good teacher. I'm

gonna be just fine."

She smiles again. "We're lucky to have found you. Let me know if there's anything you need. I'll be sure to send it your way."

And with that, I'm watching Princess Odynne glide up the stairs and into the palace, and I'm feeling even more exhausted than before.

"Hey, Bass, wanna come out with me and some friends? We can show you around."

Jai is walking toward me. I've never seen him outside of his uniform, and he's wearing red pants that are like the soft fabric I have on and a black tunic and I'm liking his style.

"Bass?" I ask, looking at him like he's crazy.

"Yeah, everyone is buzzing about the Ambassadors that are here, so I thought 'Bass' was fitting. Come on, aren't you tired of being cooped up in the palace?"

And it's like he's reading my mind because the last thing I want to do is go back to the suite and see Mia who somehow found her journal. Once again, I'm not speaking to her. I don't even want to think about her. A part of me wants to go find Evora and try Aveth again, but I decide I probably should give her some space.

"Are you gonna feed me?" I smile.

"I'm sure I can find you something."

And so, before I know it, we're walking around the Oasis city and it's honestly pretty lit. It kind of reminds me of some marketplaces Dad took us to in downtown LA before Zoey. There's a lot of people that live here in the Oasis, and it's like America in that there are a lot of different races and people who look like they come from all over the world. There are foods I've never seen before, and everything smells really good. I'm starving, and I'm kind of tired of the fancy food from the palace, and I'm wishing I could find just a bag of Doritos.

This place is definitely Jai's stomping ground. He totally knows this city, and a lot of people know him. Jai's taller than I am, and he has short dark hair. He's a lot bigger than I am, like he definitely works out. I'm hoping he'll lift with me, or show me whatever he does out here in the desert to stay fit, and I wonder if they play soccer here, or what they do for fun. He kind of reminds me of Rodrigo. We walk along the various merchant stalls.

"How's Aveth training going?"

Really bad, but I can't tell him that. "Really good. Like, I'm starting to shoot fire and stuff."

"Really?" He looks at me, and you'd think I'd like swallow uncomfortably or something or look away, but I'm really good at this kind of stuff.

So, I smile instead and say, "Yeah. Evora says I'm a real natural."

"Hey, that's awesome. We're gonna need your skills in the upcoming battles."

"For sure," I say confidently. I change the subject. "So, where are these friends of yours?"

"We're meeting them at one of my favorite places to eat. They're gonna love you."

"What do you guys do for fun around here, when you're not working?"

"We just hang out, mostly. What about you?"

"I play soccer."

"What's soccer?"

"This game with a ball and a net."

"Sounds dumb."

"Yeah, I guess it is," I agree. I guess it does for someone who doesn't understand. "Where do you live?"

"I'll show you."

"Are your parents home?"

"Don't have any. I live alone."

"What?" I'm shocked. I thought we were about the same age. "You look young. How old are you?"

"Eighteen. You're fifteen, right?"

"Almost sixteen." Which isn't really true, since I turn

sixteen in December, but whatever.

"Parents died years ago. Been alone for a long time. I've learned to make it on my own."

"Dang. That's tough. I feel for you, man."

"You gotta do what you gotta do to survive."

And then we're turning a corner and we run right into this old man. He stinks really bad and he's got a gross looking beard and it's freaky because he only has one eye and he's singing off tune and his teeth are yellow.

Jai isn't having it. "Hey, watch where you're going," he snaps, pushing the old man to the ground. The guy's cane goes flying, and I'm glad Jai pushed him, because he was gross and creepy.

The man is mumbling something as he struggles to get up. Then he looks at us and pulls out this gross cup thing. "Please, if you could spare anything. I could sing for you. A coin for a song?"

Jai just laughs at him and walks away, so I do too, but I can tell the guy's eye is still staring at me as we leave.

"Are there a lot of homeless here?" I ask, after the sound of the guy's weird song is lost in the noise of the city.

"I dunno. I don't really pay attention to that kind of stuff."

I laugh, because I don't know what to say. "Yeah, me either."

"The Emperor is the best, Bass. We're living pretty."

Before I know it, we're in some kind of tavern or something, and Jai orders something to drink. The guy behind the table gives it to him, and he offers it to me, after taking a sip.

"What is it?" I ask.

"Something we're probably too young to drink." He winks. "But I have friends in high places."

I've never drank or smoked or anything like that. No one has ever asked me to. I mean, everyone knows I'm good. I'm involved in church and I go to Sabbath School. There are some other guys from other schools I know who do that kind of stuff, but my dad would kill me if he found out and I'd never do anything that could get me kicked off the team. I can tell Jai is waiting for me to respond, and I don't know what to do. And I'm about to reach for the cup when a group of guys appear laughing loudly and Jai is now hugging them. It's like they've all known each other for years and I'm suddenly terrified I'm going to be left out again, so I'm smiling and trying to pay attention to what they're talking about. Before I know it, they surround me and Jai is introducing me to Tal, Zee, and Mardo. They're all drinking and I still haven't touched the stuff, and he's telling them I attacked a Horn Terror and that I can use Aveth now and I'm going along with it. Now they're making fun of Ralik, cause I guess they know who he is, and I'm imitating his dumb voice to make them laugh, and they talk about girls they like and I'm talking about Courtney, my "girlfriend," and they're teaching me a game of cards. The hours go by and I still haven't touched the stuff, even though when Jai asked if I liked it, I lie and say yeah it was great. We order food and it tastes alright. I'm getting tired, but I'm not sure how to get back to the palace on my own, and it's super dark now, but it doesn't seem like this night is ever going to end.

So, I get up and tell them I need to go the bathroom, which they call "the springs," and it's basically like the plumbing we have but it's hard to explain. But I go outside and into the streets, away from the noise of the tavern, the singing, the laughing and the drinking, and I'm looking for a moment of peace. I look to the sky. Man, you know what, if Dad or Tracy knew I was with these guys it would be over. I'm feeling kind of weird like I don't know how to feel, and then I'm annoyed because I realize if I ever was with people like them at home, Dad would be so busy, he'd never know anyway. I wish I had found out where Lucius lives cause I want to meet his wife and kid, but I was so caught up in wanting to get Jai to like me, I never asked. Now I'm sitting against the back wall of the tavern and it's kind of chilly out here. I'm reminded of the cold nights we spent in the desert heading here in the first place and how it's crazy all of this is even happening.

I can't be what they need me to be; I don't even know where to begin. Maybe I should go back to the square and keep training. I need faith to use Aveth—faith in the Emperor, but I've never met him. So how is that even possible? I'm supposed to look inside myself? How do I even do that? When I'm alone and think about who I am, it's super dark and confusing. I've pretended to be so many things. When I stop and *really* think about it, I'm not even sure what's in there, and maybe it doesn't even actually matter. Maybe that's what growing up is supposed to be like. I hate thinking about this deep stuff, and I don't have time for it. I just want a soccer ball, and now I'm grumpy and I'd do anything for my Apple Music and PS4. If I think about it enough, Mia's slap still stings, and maybe I just need to go to bed and this will all go away. I'm sure if I ask someone for directions to the palace they can point me there. So, I'm standing and moving, and then I feel really stupid, because I can see the giant palace in the distance and I realize if I just move in its direction, I'll eventually get there.

I stop.

I can't just leave without saying anything to Jai; the guys will think I'm weird. So I go back inside and try to tell Jai, but he's having the time of his life, so I tell Tal or Zee or one of them, and they don't really pay attention and then I'm back outside walking the dark streets of the Oasis city.

I'm trying to warm myself up as I walk, and maybe I can use Aveth after all. I start thinking about myself and who I am. I think about Grandpa and how he asked who I want to be. I think about faith in God, and realize, maybe, I'm not really sure what that looks like. Then I think about my mom and how mad I am at her, how I've been mad for years but have been unable to say how I really feel. It was all her fault. All of it was. But I'm proud of myself, because in spite of her, I've grown into someone pretty cool. I'm smart. I'm popular. I have good friends. I make good grades. I'm on the soccer team. I have a girlfriend, well, I used to. People like me. I didn't need Mom before. I don't need her now. I don't need anyone. I can be like Jai, and figure things out on my own. And part of me wishes I really had tried that drink, and I'm going to get stronger and bigger and faster and I'm going to be better than they ever imagined because I can do anything if I set my mind to it. Faith? I can have faith in *myself*. I look down, and my fingers are tingling, and warmth is coming from them. Am I going crazy, or are the tips of my fingers turning red and orange? *Is this Aveth?*

I look up and there he is again. The crazy man with one eye. I'm about to turn away, because no way am I going to give him *anything* if he starts begging, but I stop, because that's not what is happening.

He's bending down and I didn't notice them before, but there are two little homeless kids holding each other against the side of the building, trying to protect themselves from the cold.

I watch as this old man, who has *nothing*, is giving them the thin, dirty, blanket he had wrapped around himself, and then he's dumping all of the little he earned that day from his cup begging in the marketplace on the ground before the kids. Every. Single. Coin

And I'm trying to focus on the Aveth as I hear him mumble, "But Ruach forgives, and pays the cost, the true king returns that which was lost…"

His eye meets mine again, as I'm running away.

Chapter 9
Study Questions

1. Why is it important to surround yourself with good friends? How do you go about making sure you are friends with people who make you a better person?

2. Have you ever felt pressured by friends to do something you knew was wrong? What did you do? How can you make good decisions when you're around your friends?

3. Have you ever been upset with your parents? What do you do? Who can you talk to about it?

4. Oliver immediately points out Odynne is less attractive than Evora. He mentions her nose, in particular, something she has no control over. Is it hurtful to judge people based on how they look? Does God do this?

5. Oliver comes to the conclusion in this chapter that he doesn't need anyone; he can do things on his own. Is this a healthy way to think? Why?

6. Read Hebrews 11:6. How could this apply to Oliver and his experience so far?

Chapter 10:
So, My Questions Have Questions
Mia

Well, we have now left the Oasis and are back in the desert on the way to Kaalinon. This time it's all of us who were traveling before, plus an entire army tagging along to, I guess, occupy the bad guy kingdom. I asked Evora if they did the same thing with Canterbor, and she said they are not as strong of a force as Kaalinon. Which is surprising. If those crazy scary guys are the *weak* ones, I am sure not looking forward to the strong ones.

We also have a lot of supplies, which we didn't have last time. But Kaalinon is apparently super cold so we have coats and furs (gross, I am not okay with those) and blankets and tents now.

Have I ever mentioned that I'm not a super huge fan of the cold? I've spent more than a few Christmases in Michigan thanks to my *abuelos*, and I guess the sledding and snowman making can be fun, but at what cost? Catching pneumonia? The loss of fingers and toes? Having to take ten minutes to put on all the layers? Already the desert heat is tapering off and I can feel the cold air coming.

Speaking of cold, Oliver's cold shoulder is about all I've gotten from him. He's got his little posse of friends now, he always does, and I'm just here off to the side. He's strutting around like a baboon thinking he's all that with Jai and Linnetia. And showing off to Evora.

Although he didn't say it straight to me, apparently he's great at Aveth? I haven't seen him do anything but talk about it though so I'm thinking maybe it's like that time that Oliver insisted he was going through puberty, but I was still taller than him and his "deep" voice was clearly fake.

I'm kind of wondering why Evora hasn't started training me too. I mean she practically said that I'm the real Ambassador anyway. Maybe she wants to give him a shot before kicking him out.

Or maybe I'm the mistake.

I don't want to think about that.

Evora's horse joins mine. "How are you faring?" she asks politely.

"Oh, I'm fine. I'm good."

"Did you like Rukin?"

"Oh, totally! Your home is way cooler than mine." Ugh, why am I always so awkward?

"I'd like to see yours sometime."

This brings up a question. "So, can you go through the portal the other direction? Does it work both ways?"

"No," she says. "It was only designed for Ambassadors to go between."

"Designed by who?" I tilt my head.

"Oh," she answers quickly, "it was long ago. I don't know."

Hmm. "Okay…" I seem to have made the princess uncomfortable. But I was only asking a question, so I'm not sure why. "Do y'all have a God or something?" I think about the God I grew up learning about in Sabbath School. I don't know how I feel about that guy anyway. People in the church haven't always been very nice to me. And some of their beliefs seem weird and outdated. But still, if someone asks if I believe in God, I would say yes because the whole idea of creation and stuff makes sense to me.

So, back to my question about whoever designed the portals.

"A what?" She asks, confused.

"Like, someone who set up the whole world to be the way it is?" I'm not sure how to explain the concept.

"I…I don't know," she shakes her head. Evora is looking at

me strangely. She pauses a moment, then asks, "Did you talk to anyone outside of the palace?"

"No," I lie. There was that one kooky man with the weird song.

"Why are you asking so many questions?"

"Because I'm curious and I'm not from here."

"Well, they are unimportant-"

"-I was just asking-"

"-Just drop it," she commands kind of loudly.

"Sorry," I mumble to her back as she speeds up the horse and leaves me behind.

I reach into my backpack and pull out my journal. I wrote down that song so I wouldn't forget it since it made me feel all sorts of strange ways.

There's stuff about the Blight, which I haven't heard mentioned, and stuff about Ruach, another foreign word. I circle them both and put a question mark beside them. I decide to ask somebody else, not Evora, about them sometime.

Late in the afternoon, we stop to make camp for the night. Some people get supper started, others set up camp (remember, there's a whole army with us now), and I decide to take Estrellita for a walk because she gets pretty bored riding on a horse all day. Plus, I want to stretch my legs.

It's pretty safe here in Rukin. So as long as I don't get myself lost in the endless desert hills, I should be fine. Plus, this dog is feisty.

I keep on the lookout for Horn Terrors.

I'm wandering and I'm thinking about how weird Evora was acting. What did I do to deserve that, and how come she's training Oliver in Aveth but not me, if I'm the real chosen Ambassador and he's just a fraud? And what did that guy mean in his song about scarred hearts and scarred land? Was he just crazy and I'm obsessing over nothing, or was there something to it? Why am I still thinking about it? Why did it seem kind of familiar?

Lost in my thoughts, I am startled to run into Oliver and

Jai as I climb over a sand dune.

"What are you doing here?" Oliver accuses me, as if I have just been caught trying to break into a bank vault.

"Chill, I'm just on a walk," I snap. At least he's talking to me, right? "What are you doing?"

"Hunting," Jai answers.

I look behind them, look behind me, and raise an eyebrow. "Hunting...sand?" We are, as far as I can tell, the only creatures for miles.

"Don't act like you know how to hunt in the desert," Oliver rolls his eyes.

"Oh, and you do, Mr. Macho?"

"I live in the desert."

"You live in *San Diego*."

"It's the desert!"

"It's the city."

"Shut up!" he growls.

It's the most we've said to each other in days.

The sun is going down now, and I'm starting to get cold. Oliver pushes past me with Jai.

"Fine," I say. "Leave. You've had plenty of practice."

He doesn't stop walking.

Pretty soon, Jai and Oliver's heads disappear behind a sand dune, and I decide to return to the camp, fuming. I imagine smoke coming out of my ears.

I haven't gone very far when I hear a shout from Oliver's voice and the unsettling clanging of metal against metal. Uh-oh. Maybe another scary beast?

I look in the direction of the camp. Should I run and get help? Another scream, this one Jai's, has me running toward the sounds instead. Whatever is going on, they are in immediate danger, and if I leave now, it might be too late.

I climb over a hill to find, not a Horn Terror, but those persistent Canterbor soldiers again. There are just a few, and they are led by my old friend, the kid with the scar. He is with a woman with skin about the same color as mine, and a young woman with skin that is very dark.

All in a moment, I see Jai lying unconscious on the ground, and the Canterbor guy throwing my brother to the ground.

"Hey!" I shout.

Why did I do that? I'm only armed with a small terrier.

And suddenly, the other two soldiers are coming toward me, and I'm backing up, but tripping because walking on sand isn't easy, especially backwards. I let go of the leash, and Estrellita runs away. Thanks for protecting me, dog. I thought we had a good relationship.

They grab me, one arm each. I scream as loud as I can. Oh, please let someone at the camp hear me.

I'm pulled to where Oliver has been smashed into the ground. "Listen to me!" the soldier grunts as Oliver tries to fight. Oliver doesn't have a chance, even with the soldier still in a sling.

And then, wonder upon wonders, Oliver wasn't lying after all.

All at once, his hands glow, the guy holding him down rips his hand away, and I see old burns up his forearms. I also see all the color drain out of his face. "It's too late," he mutters. I just barely hear him because I'm so entranced with Oliver shooting fire out of his hands, and I wonder if it really is him and not me after all.

The soldier looks into my eyes searchingly for a moment, and I see that they are blue and that he's maybe seen a lot. "Just her," he commands the women holding me.

They begin to pull me away, and I struggle, but they're strong, and...

And Oliver comes to my rescue.

The fire comes out of his hands again, right in our direction, and I'm gonna be so mad if Oliver burns me to a crisp trying to save me.

But the kid with the scar...blocks it?

His right hand is extended, and he looks scared but determined. He's not countering Oliver's fire with fire. It's some invisible force, like wind, but maybe not quite like wind, and it creates a bubble around us so we can't get burned. And the fire dies away.

Oliver looks at his hands in surprise and confusion.

"What was that?" I can't help but ask.

"Ruach," the soldier whispers, looking me in the eyes again.

And suddenly I have so many more questions.

But I hear galloping horses, and arrows start flying, and I spot Estrellita, the best of dogs, leading the cavalry to rescue us.

The three Canterbor soldiers seem to remember that they are in enemy territory and that their stealth mission has gone south. They retreat, and I don't see where they went, but I see Rukin soldiers looking for them as well. I guess the bad guys lost again. I guess the bad guys got away.

I guess we've been rescued. I guess we're safe now. I guess I have nothing to fear since Evora is protecting us. Now that the Emperor is protecting us.

I guess.

...Right?

Chapter 10
Study Questions

1. Mia thinks that some parts of her church are weird and outdated. Have you ever experienced that? Did you do anything about it?

2. Oliver and Mia are not treating each other well. What does 1 Peter 1:22 say about how we should treat each other?

3. How was Oliver able to use Aveth? Did it have to do with faith, or something else?

4. Mia begins to have misgivings about what she has been told. Read Hebrews 5:11-14. How can you learn to tell what is true and what is a lie?

Chapter 11:
So, Don't Ask Me Because I Don't Know Oliver

Don't even ask how I used Aveth, because I have no idea. One minute some dude in green is trying to tie me up, and the next I'm shooting fire out of my hands. And the only time I even came close to that before was that night in the Oasis city when my hands were warm and tingly and red and orange and if I had a marshmallow, I would have toasted it. So, yeah, after that, it was like I had just singlehandedly won a soccer game 6-0. Jai was sure to tell everyone how amazing I was, and I'm totally a legend now at 15. I was basically signing autographs, and I wanted my first autograph to be on Mia's face. Wanna know my secret? I have no idea how I even did it. And yeah, that kind of worries me. Because if we're about to face down an entire army of ice soldiers. I'm thinking fire will come in very handy, and because now it's clear that I'm the chosen one, I'm definitely feeling the pressure.

"I'm proud of you." Evora is staring at me a few days later. We're still in the desert, and it's rockier and less sandy this far north in Elior, but still very hot in the day and very cold at night. People are getting off their horses and we're making camp again.

"Hey, thanks, I have the best of teachers." I smile back, and I'm not gonna lie, Evora had been kind of distant with me the past few days after leaving the Oasis city. I tried to pretend like I didn't really care because I had my group of friends and maybe if I acted like I didn't care about her, she'd miss me more? I dunno. It always worked with Courtney. But ever since I toasted that guy, she's been glued to my side.

"Aveth is the only way we'll get close to that portal. You and I, together." She reaches out and squeezes my hand and I gladly take it and squeeze back. I'm nodding now and swallowing, and my throat is dry. Her hand is so soft and so cool. "We really need one more to make sure you seal it." I follow her gaze over to Mia who is with Ralik, helping him set up his tent. "Soldier!" Evora commands, and suddenly he's standing at attention. Mia looks surprised.

"Your Highness," Ralik responds in that funny-sounding-voice of his.

I look for Jai so we can laugh about it, but I don't see him.

"Set up your own tent," she snaps. "I need the Ambassador to begin her training." And now Evora is staring at Mia.

"Oh, I really don't mind helping him," Mia says quickly, and now a few soldiers are watching. There's Linnetia. She smirks at me. I smirk back.

"We really should begin, Mia. We could use another Aveth user at the portal."

Mia approaches her and softens her voice. "But Ralik could really use help with his tent." She pauses, "It kind of takes him longer than the others."

"If a soldier can't set up a simple tent, maybe I should reevaluate his worth in my army."

Now, Mia and Evora are staring at each other and it just got awkward, and what is Mia doing? Like, we're the Ambassadors and Evora needs us. She told us this from the very beginning. Why is Mia being so stupid? I glare at her. She's such a child.

Mia's tone sharpens. "I'm going to help Ralik. I'll look for you later." And then she turns around and walks back to Ralik who smiles weakly at her. The guy is so lame. Why is he even here?

I look at Evora. "Sorry about that."

"I guess there's no question about who was *actually* supposed to come through the portal." She puts her hand on my face and now I have chills. "Thanks for caring."

"Of course," I stutter, looking into her perfect eyes. "Whatever you need."

"Let's train more tonight."

"I'll find you."

She nods and heads away and I could literally soar through the sky; I'm so hyped. And before I know it, I'm out hunting with Jai in the desert, which is basically just us working out together. He shoots a couple of sand critters here and there with his bow and arrows. By the way, I am a terrible shot, but nobody needs to know that. We laugh and talk about dumb stuff and just goof off.

"Have you ever been in a really big battle?" I ask as we're heading back to camp.

"Not like huge, but I have been in a battle."

"What's it like?"

"Chaos." His eyes flicker. "I love it."

"Guess it's useful to have Evora's Aveth."

"Yeah. Definitely makes it easier."

"Can *anyone* use it?"

Jai shrugs. "I don't know. I don't think so, or we'd all do it, right? I think you have to be chosen somehow."

"By who?"

"Something to do with the Emperor. He's lived hundreds of years. He's really powerful."

"Have you ever met him?"

"Just once. But I think now that I'm with Evora, I'll get a chance to really know him. You for sure will. I know this battle for the portal will be huge. I wouldn't be surprised if the Emperor brings his own Shadim to fight in the battle."

"His what?"

"The Shadim. They are like his elite guard. Super formidable. Almost like, unbeatable. They have amazing power."

"Have you ever seen them fight?"

"I've only heard stories. Bass, they're ridiculously strong." He's smiling, and I'm getting really excited at the chance of meeting the Emperor and fighting alongside his Shadim. Well, if I can learn how to really control Aveth, instead of it, like, just happening. Okay, maybe that's more nerves than excitement. I don't really know.

"Don't you think I need to learn how to fight with a sword too? Just in case?"

"In case what?" Jai looks confused.

In case my Aveth doesn't work, but I can't say that. "In case someone wants to duel the Ambassador. I don't wanna look stupid if I don't know how to fight."

"Just blast them with fire."

I laugh and change the subject. I meant to train with Lucius, but I didn't see him at all in the Oasis city and haven't seen him since we left.

We get back to camp and Jai disappears with Linnetia and Cerise. I find myself with nothing to do, so I take a little walk around camp. As I walk by, most people wave or try to talk to me. I'm not gonna lie, I'm loving it. Like, at school, I'm not the guy everyone is wanting to talk to. I have my group of friends, but I'm not popular like the starters on the basketball team or the best guys in soccer. I wish I was, and I try really hard to be like them. But I'm just not as good as them and it's really frustrating. Here, I'm appreciated, and it's about time.

I see Mia writing in her journal and she doesn't notice me. For a second, I wonder what it would have been like if we had stayed together. If she would have come with me and Dad to California. If things would have been different. It's weird because she's my sister, but I barely know her. She's the kid that has to prove to everyone how different she is. Why? I'm not sure. But it's super obnoxious, and a little funny, because no one really cares here. When I walk by, people say, "Hi Oliver." I wonder what they do when she walks by. For a moment I want to go up to her and see how she's doing, but then I remember she lost my phone, she slapped me in the face, and she's been just ridiculous since we got here. I walk by and say nothing. Instead I laugh really loudly with some of the soldiers who come up to talk to me. I'm eyeing Mia to see if she's watching, and she doesn't ever look up. Not even once. Whatever, Mia.

"Excuse me, Oliver?"

Ralik is standing before me with his big goofy grin. I roll my eyes. I really don't wanna talk to him. "What?" I say, not stopping, and walking around him.

"Thanks for training so hard. Thanks for learning Aveth."

"Yeah," I say quickly, but I don't make eye contact. Instead I'm looking around to see if anyone is watching me talk to this guy. I'm hoping not.

"I'm glad you're with us," he's saying, and he's following me. I'm trying to walk faster, and I'm waving back at some soldiers as I move away.

And there's Lucius, and my heart swells, because I've missed him so much. Out of everyone I've met here, he's really the one I've wanted to talk to about everything. I want him to know I used Aveth and I want him to be proud of me. I'm smiling at him, but he looks right past me and moves to Ralik. I watch as Lucius hugs him. "How has it been going, my friend?" he asks Ralik.

Ralik smiles bigger than I've seen before. "Good. Glad you're back."

Lucius nods and slaps his big hand on Ralik's back. "It's good to see you."

"Is Vyn okay?" Ralik asks.

"He's comfortable." Lucius looks down. "It was hard to leave them."

"I'm sorry."

"It's okay. I do it for them." Then Lucius is looking at me. He smiles and pulls me into a hug too. "And how's the famous Ambassador? Should I start calling you Firefingers?"

I laugh. "I mean, if you want." And hugging him feels good. Honestly, hugging anyone feels good, and I swallow down a lump in my throat because I miss my dad and I wonder if they've called the cops by now.

"Eat dinner with me tonight, Ralik," Lucius smiles at him. "I need to speak to Oliver now."

"Okay," Ralik laughs excitedly. I look at him, and he seems so happy, and for the first time, I see him differently. I can't explain it, but I'm starting to feel a little guilty for how I've treated him, and I would never want Lucius to see or hear the ways I've made fun of him.

Lucius puts his arm around me, and we walk a little away from camp. We find a palm tree that provides some shade and we sit down on a couple of rocks. He tosses his canteen to me and I take a sip of his water.

"I wanted to see you in the Oasis city," I begin, not sure what he wants to talk to me about. "I wanted to meet Vyn and Kessia."

"Vyn is sick." Lucius looks at me, and he suddenly looks way older and way sadder than I've noticed before.

"What do you mean?"

"He was born with a condition. It's incurable, and," I can hear the sadness in Lucius's voice, and I think he's holding back tears, "well, every moment with him is precious."

I watch as Lucius looks down to collect himself and I don't wanna ask it, but I can't help myself. "Then why are you out here?"

"His treatments are expensive. They won't save his life, but they'll make him more comfortable."

And I think back to 4th grade when my classmate Darren's mom died of cancer. We were all at the funeral, and Darren's dad had to get up there to talk about her. Everyone was crying. Darren had to sit in the front of the church, and the school's choir sang. I will never forget looking at that coffin at the front of the church, and wondering what happens after we die and hoping I'd never have to go through something like that. I remember inching closer to my mom in the pew and hugging her a little bit tighter that night before I went to sleep.

I wonder how long Vyn has left to live, but I figure I won't ask Lucius that. There's not much I can do or say to make him feel better. "I'm sorry," I say, and I wish I could do more.

"Evora's family pays me well to be here. After you close the portal, hopefully I can go back and spend more time with them."

"Hopefully," I respond, and now I'm feeling even worse, because if Vyn is sick and Ralik is...different too, maybe that's why Lucius makes sure that Ralik is always okay. If Lucius finds out how mean I've been to him, he'll probably hate me.

"I wanted to talk to you." Lucius is staring at me, and I'm

terrified it's about Ralik.

"Okay," I sit up straighter.

"I know you must be under a lot of pressure. All of this is new to you and a lot of hope is placed on your shoulders as the Ambassador. When I heard you used Aveth," he clears his throat, "I wanted to tell you a few things."

"Okay," I say hesitantly.

He continues slowly. "Aveth takes a toll. I've watched Evora through the years, and it...does something to her. I think with great power comes great responsibility."

Suddenly I'm remembering my conversation with Odynne. "Princess Odynne said she was afraid of Aveth."

Lucius nods. "King Jethil has done a lot to preserve the Emperor's power. He is a great man, and his family has fought to protect what the Emperor has built for years. But I've seen..." he stops himself. He pauses for a moment and I'm sitting on the edge of my rock, waiting. His big eyes look sad and he looks so tired, and I wish I could hug him again. "I've seen the price that has been paid."

"What do you mean?"

"Elior is slowly dying, Oliver. The Horn Terror we faced—legend says long ago they weren't violent or fierce. They used to be loving. All the creatures of Elior were loving. Things have changed."

"Because of the Dark Prince?"

Lucius nods. "It seems Aveth is the only thing to fight him with. But sometimes I wonder if the destructive nature of Aveth has tainted Elior too."

"But isn't Aveth good?"

He pauses. "I know it's *necessary*."

His gaze is serious, and suddenly I'm a little afraid.

"I care about you, Oliver, and I want to make sure you're okay. I want to be sure that you can handle this, that I can lend you whatever support you may need. I know Evora feels the same way."

"Thank you. I'm just honestly a little overwhelmed and

confused by it all." And I want to tell Lucius the truth. I want to tell him that I don't even know how to control Aveth, that it just kind of...*happened*. But instead I say, "I love using it. I'm really good at it."

Lucius smiles. "So, I've heard. I believe what they say about the Emperor, that sometimes we must suffer for his glory. Perhaps Aveth is part of the way we must suffer. You've been chosen. I just want you to know, I'm here for you, and I'll help you get through the toll it may take on you."

And I want to get up and hug him, but I don't want to be all sappy or anything, so I smile and say, "Thanks, Lucius. Means a lot." I think of something else. "I have a question for you. When the Canterbor soldiers attacked us yesterday, one of them did this weird wind thing to me they called Ruach. Do you know anything about it?"

His face pinches into a scowl. "It's the anti-Aveth. If Aveth is unstable, Ruach is far worse. It's the Dark Prince's tool for great evil."

I sigh deeply. "So, avoid Ruach. Got it."

"Lucius, you're back," Evora runs up to us and hugs him.

"Have you been okay?" he asks her. I look at them and can tell how deeply he cares about her. He's such a good dude.

"Yes. Oliver has kept me safe." She smiles and I think she winks at me, but maybe she just blinks, and I give her thumbs up instead of saying something awesome. "Can you come with me?" she asks Lucius. "We're going over battle plans for when we reach the border of Kaalinon. I know they will be ready for us."

"In full force," Lucius adds.

"Maybe the Shadim will join us?" I chime in, and they both look at me and I smile. "Can't your dad ask the Emperor to send them our way?"

"We can only hope," Evora nods then looks at Lucius.

"Oliver, why don't you join Ralik and me during dinner?" Lucius calls out, almost knowingly, as they're heading back to camp.

"I'll be there," I smile hesitantly.

"Are you staying out here?" Evora wonders.

"Just want some alone time. I'll be back soon."

"I know you'll be safe. You can take care of yourself now."
She smiles proudly as she and Lucius walk away.

I sigh a big sigh and look at my hands. Okay, hands, make
Aveth. I point them up towards the two suns and breathe deeply. Okay. *NOW*!

And nothing happens. I don't know how long I'm out
there, but I'm hot and sweaty and my shirt is off again. It's
frustrating and I can't get it to work, and the only things that
are turning red are my nose, cheeks, and back. If they think
I can use Aveth whenever I want, then they'll probably stick
me up on the front lines to blast away the ice soldiers with my
fire powers and instead I'll be killed immediately but definitely
laughed at first.

Great. Yay me.

Point hands to the suns.

Now!

Nothing happens.

Nothing at all.

Some Ambassador I am.

Chapter 11
Study Questions

1. Have you ever pretended to be something you're not? Why? Is it important to be genuine about who you are?

2. Oliver almost goes up to Mia to see how she's doing but he chooses not to. Why? What are some reasons you don't reach out to people you're upset with? What would be some good reasons to swallow your pride and to make peace?

3. Oliver seems to show that he feels some regret about how he's treated Ralik. How can we find healing and peace with someone that may have bullied us? How can we find forgiveness for bullying others? What steps should we take, specifically with those we've hurt? With God?

4. Do you know anyone with or have you ever lost someone to a disease like cancer? Diseases like cancer are very destructive and cause a lot of hurt and pain. What are some ways you can support families who may struggle with this reality?

5. Read Hebrews 6:11-12. Sometimes we fake our faith. What advice would you give Oliver in response to what you read?

Chapter 12:
So, If Unicorns Are Real, What Else Is?
Mia

If someone had told me back in May that during the summer of 2019 I would be the Ambassador of Elior on a special mission to close an evil portal to protect the world from a Dark Prince, I would have thought they were just making fun of the weird kid. And yet, here I am.

And it doesn't seem to be working out the way I hoped it would.

For starters, Oliver has all the friends. I know, I know, that part isn't new, but I just thought...I just hoped...I don't know. I'm not feeling very chosen right about now.

And then, I'm also stuck here riding a horse in a land where there are unicorns. I've actually picked up the whole horseback riding thing pretty quickly, but apparently not well enough for them to let me take a unicorn from the oasis in Rukin. Believe me, I asked.

Sure, I can ride a horse now, that's just great. Know what Oliver can do now? *Shoot fire from his hands.* I mean, I haven't seen him do it since, and sure, he almost barbecued me as well as the bad guys, but he also kind of saved me. And he hasn't been blatantly mean to me since then, either.

We're nearing Kaalinon now, and I know this for a couple of reasons. One: It's cold enough now that we are all starting to wear more layers. I've got some thick black pants on top of some legging-type things, as well as a gray sweater over my long-sleeved cotton shirt. No need quite yet for the gloves and hats and scarves and snow boots. We are still in the desert for now. Two: Evora apparently got word from her mysterious network that there are riots going on in Kaalinon. I've learned that you can't secretly bring an army through a desert, and we did have that run-in with the soldiers from Canterbor, and I guess Canterbor and Kaalinon are on the same side. All of this is to say that the Kaalinon troops know we're coming and they're gearing up to fight for their portal.

And this is where I'm getting uncomfortable. If someone had told me back in May that I, Mia Alejandra De la Cruz, would be on the side of the empire and not the rebellion, I would say they didn't know me at all.

Something has been bugging me like when you're flying and only one of your ears pops all the way, and the other one pops a little bit but you can still tell that you haven't been able to hear everything.

Soldier-with-the-scar-guy (I feel like I should give him a name, I don't want to categorize him by just one feature, let's call him Steve, said "Ruach" when he did the whoosh of air with his hands.

But that doesn't make sense, right? Because that crazy old guy said, *"But Ruach forgives, and pays the cost. The true king returns that which was lost."* That doesn't sound like a bad thing, and at first I thought that maybe Ruach was another word for Aveth. But I know what Aveth looks like and it wasn't that.

I decide I need to get out of my head, so I catch my horse up with Lucius who is riding a bit ahead.

"Hey."

He looks at me and smiles. "How are you feeling, Ambassador?"

"Confused," I tell him. Usually when people ask how you are, they just want to hear "Fine" or "Great" so they can forget about you and move on with their day. But I think Lucius really wants to know.

"About your role in all this?" Lucius gestures to the desert around him.

"Yeah, but some other stuff."

"Anything I can help you with?"

I'm glad you asked, Lucius, I'm glad you asked. "Can you tell me about Ruach?" I say nonchalantly.

His back stiffens. "Who told you about Ruach?"

"I hear stuff," I shrug.

"It's the counterfeit of Aveth," he tells me. "A distortion of the Dark Prince."

"So, if you follow the Dark Prince, you can use it?" I ask.

"I suppose." He swallows. "I'm sorry. I'm not too comfortable talking about this."

"That bad, huh?"

"That bad," he agrees.

I make a mental note to write down *"Ruach: Distortion of Aveth"* under my list about the Dark Prince.

While Lucius was honest, he still doesn't make that twist in my stomach go away. I spot Cerise up ahead and ask her about the Dark Prince. I'm not as subtle as I probably should have been and the others around us glance at her uncomfortably.

She looks into my eyes. "I don't enjoy discussing him. But for you, Ambassador, I will say this: He is proud. He is cruel. He is deceitful. He is the antithesis of the Emperor."

DARK PRINCE (UPDATED)
• Unjust
• Selfish
• Cruel
• Terrifying
• Ruach (Distortion of Aveth)****
• Scary

"Antithesis?"

"The exact opposite," Cerise clarifies.

"I see." Something about this definitely rings true, and I don't know why. I'll add that to my list, too.

"But, what about…"

"Mia, there you are. When are we going to start training you in Aveth?" Evora interrupts my thoughts.

Okay, I may have been avoiding Evora for the last several days. She keeps wanting me to train, and it's what I wanted before, but I'm hesitant now, and I don't know why.

"Tonight?" She asks me. Something about her tone makes me uncomfortable.

"Yep, totally." This isn't true in the least, but I just want to get away from her.

"Perfect," she smiles, eyeing me. "After dinner?"

"Mmhhmm."

What? I'm not as good at lying as Oliver.

I find myself dreading the moment we stop to set up camp for the night. What is wrong with me? Why don't I want to learn Aveth? I've seen how it works. I've seen that it's real. I know that I have to learn how to use it in order to be the hero.

But I can't get Steve's face out of my mind. Everyone says they're trying to kill Oliver and me. But we've run into him, like, three times now, and we're still alive. And he was trying to tie Oliver up, not kill him.

I almost wish I could just sit Steve down and get his side of the story.

The light fades behind the sand dunes and we stop for the night. My heart starts racing as I frantically hop off my horse and duck behind a newly popped up tent, hoping Evora doesn't spot me in the dark. I won hide-and-seek one time at school. It was because everybody forgot I was playing, but I still won.

After the incident with Steve and his friends, Oliver and I aren't allowed to leave the camp for our own safety. This is just a little problem since I'm left with not a lot of places to hide. But the camp is big and I can make myself small. Just avoid Evora until the morning, Mia.

"What are you doing?"

I jump, and notice Ralik watching me. Guess I'm not as sneaky as I thought. "Just...relaxing." I try to casually lean my back against the tent.

"Are you hiding from the princess?" he asks curiously.

"Who wants to know?"

"Me."

"Okay, fine," I whisper, standing up. "I don't want her to teach me Aveth."

"Why not? Don't you want to be important?"

"It's all I want," I mutter. "But sometimes being different isn't all it's cracked up to be."

"I know," Ralik answers.

I guess he does.

I tilt my head. "Ralik, what do you know about Ruach and the Dark Prince?"

"My dad says the Dark Prince is scary," Ralik tells me. "But I think the Emperor is scary, too."

Well, that's interesting. "Scary how?"

"I've never met him. But Jai did one time. It was all he could talk about for a while. Jai used to be nice. He's not anymore."

"Because he met the Emperor?"

Ralik's mind is now somewhere else and he leaves me alone with my thoughts.

Until I hear Princess Evora's voice not too far away. I sneak from tent to tent, trying to stay in the shadows. I settle by a supply carriage. But then my stomach growls and I remember that I haven't eaten supper. I look longingly toward one of the fires where Cerise sits feeding Estrellita scraps from her plate. But Evora is right there too, talking to a couple of attendants, and I can't risk it. I'm starting to feel really silly right about now. And hangry. You know, hungry and angry.

"What are you doing?" I hear for the second time tonight.

I whip around, my back to the carriage. This time it's Oliver, standing there wrapped in a wool blanket. His pants are brown and he is wearing leather boots that look surprisingly in style back home, and a maroon shirt. If he was wearing orange, he might blend in with the soldiers.

"Why do you care?"

"I don't," he says quickly. "But Ralik told me to come over here. I don't know why I listened."

He's standing there awkwardly with a plate of food in his hand.

"Okay, bye," he turns to go.

"I'm afraid to learn Aveth." There. I said it.

103

Oliver stares at me for a moment. "Because you're worried you won't be as good at it as me?"

I roll my eyes. "Calm down, your little friends aren't around right now. You don't need to show off."

Oliver looks around and takes a deep breath. "Evora is just trying to help you. Why are you being so weird about it? Why do you have to be so weird about everything?"

"How do you know that, though?" I whisper. "I mean, what do we really know about her? About any of this? What does she gain from making us close the portal?"

"Um, a safe kingdom. Duh."

Fair point, she's been pretty open about that. "But what about Ruach?"

Oliver sucks in his breath. What I said looks like it's affecting him the same way as that one time he got stung on the nose by a wasp. "We're not supposed to talk about Ruach."

"So, you heard what he said, too. Oliver, Steve hasn't tried to kill us at all. And he could have just a few days ago."

"Who's Steve?"

"You know who I'm talking about," I insist. I sit down on the cool sand and beckon Oliver to join me. I half expect him to walk away instead, but he uncomfortably sits a couple feet away from me.

"All I know is that Evora isn't bad, Mia. And neither is Aveth." He seems pretty sure. But he's also not the sharpest crayon in the box, so I'm still not sure I believe him.

"What did it feel like when you used it?" I wonder.

He considers my question for a moment. "Strong. Like I could do anything."

Well, that doesn't sound so bad. I could use some strength right about now. "Can you show me?" I reach toward his hand.

He jerks it away. "I don't need to prove anything to you."

"Okay...touchy," I mutter.

"Look," Oliver says as he runs his hands through his hair. "Evora says there are stages to mastering Aveth. You have to have faith in yourself, and then satisfaction in your work, and perseverance, and some other stuff that I don't exactly remember. It's not bad stuff though."

I don't answer, and instead, lean my head against the carriage wheel. We just sit in silence for a few minutes, and it's strange but kind of nice. My stomach growling awkwardly breaks the silence, and after a bit of hesitation, Oliver hands me his half-eaten plate of food.

I accept it, but before I start chowing down, I say timidly, "I'm sorry for losing your phone and slapping you and stuff."

He nods and looks down. Now would be a good time to apologize for being mean and throwing my journal out a window, Oliver.

"Sometimes, Mia, I wonder how we got here. 'Cause, think about it. We say we're sorry and say we're sorry and nothing ever changes."

"You're right," I say. "I wish you weren't."

"Me too."

What must it be like to have a family that isn't so broken? "So, our pact," I say slowly, "the one we made your first night at Lito and Lita's. To just get through it and go our separate ways…"

"Just because we're here doesn't mean anything is different," he says, and I look for a hint of sadness in his eyes.

Oliver sighs and stands up. "Keep the food. I'll cover for you with Evora tonight, but that's it."

"The true king returns that which was lost," I whisper.

"Huh?"

"It's just something I heard." I pick at a loose thread on the cuff of my pants.

"The true king? You mean the Emperor?"

"I don't know," I sigh. "But someone out there can help us change. Can fix…this." I point to him, then to me.

Oliver raises an eyebrow. "I thought you weren't religious."

I smirk. "Well, I didn't think there were unicorns either."

Oliver leaves me, and as I munch on his food, I think back to

105

a time when maybe I did have faith. When I believed everything they taught me in Sabbath School. Before Dad and Oliver and my friends and God left. Because that's the thing. Everyone leaves.

I take out my journal and begin copying down all the new words I learned about the Dark Prince today. Ruach: Distortion of Aveth. Opposite of the Emperor. Scary.

I just wish I could know. I wish I could know for sure that I'm on the right side. That the Emperor is good. That the Dark Prince is bad.

As I close the journal, the note written on the first page catches my eye. Now, this is something a lot of people don't know, but my dad is actually the one who gave me this journal. It was a lot of years ago, before the divorce, and he knew I liked to doodle and write and stuff. It was just a silly stocking stuffer one year at Christmas, and I don't even know why I kept it, but when my counselor told me to start journaling my thoughts this was the one I found.

This is what the note says:

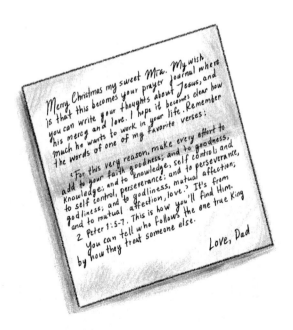

Merry Christmas my sweet Mira. My wish is that this becomes your prayer journal where you can write your thoughts about Jesus, and his mercy and love. I hope it becomes clear how much he wants to work in your life. Remember the words of one of my favorite verses:

'For this very reason, make every effort to add to your faith goodness, and to goodness, knowledge; and to knowledge, self control; and to self control, perseverance; and to perseverance, godliness; and to godliness, mutual affection; and to mutual affection, love.' It's from 2 Peter 1:5-7. This is how you'll find Him. You can tell who follows the one true King by how they treat someone else.

Love, Dad

The one true king. It means something to my Dad in my world, but what about here? Is there really something to this faith thing? I wonder what that looks like here in Elior.

I flip through the pages of my journal to find a blank one. I write *ONE TRUE KING???* at the top. I don't have anything to write under it yet. But I'll be on the lookout.

Chapter 12
Study Questions

1. Cerise tells Mia that the Dark Prince is the antithesis, or the exact opposite, of the Emperor. Do you believe her? Do you think Mia believes her?

2. Why doesn't Mia want to start training in Aveth? Have you ever really wanted something, but it turned out to not be as good as you thought it would be?

3. Read Hebrews 7:25-28. Can God be scary and still good?

4. Mia's dad mentions 2 Peter 1:5-7. Read it for yourself. What do you think it means? How can you recognize a follower of Jesus?

Chapter 13:
So, Pluto is More Popular Than Me
Oliver

Why does she always have to do that? Whenever she isn't the center of attention, she has to rain on everyone else's parade. If Mia was the one shooting fire out of her hands, I'm sure she'd be preaching about how Aveth was the best thing ever. But just because I can, and she *can't*, of *course* I'm the bad guy. I wrap my blanket around me tighter, because honestly, it's like zero degrees. I hate the cold and I'm not feelin' it. I keep seeing that creepy one-eyed dude in my head, and I hear that weird word, Ruach, over and over again, and I see myself pointing stupidly at the suns with no results, and Mia becoming queen of Elior. I just want to go to sleep.

To make matters worse, for some reason Pluto keeps following me around and trying to lick my ankles. She's such a weird dog and the most popular member of Team Ambassador. She's melting the hearts of all of these "tough" soldiers, and I don't understand what's so great about the dog. She smells. She barks all the time. She eats. She sleeps. She "marks her territory" literally everywhere. Yay Pluto. Now I'm imagining them crowning Mia queen and then making Pluto the princess with a stupid dog crown.

Speak of the devil, here comes her majesty running in circles around Linnetia, who is laughing.

"I love her so much," she swoons.

I put on my best smile, the one that fools them all. "Where's Jai?"

"With some of the guys. They're playing cards."

They didn't invite me. That stinks. "Where?"

But Linnetia isn't listening. She's sitting in the sand and

Pluto is on her lap licking her face. So gross. That tongue has literally been everywhere. I keep walking.

The moon is up high in the sky, and it's huge, like one of those big white moons you see in video games when you're riding your horse for miles and miles. Okay, maybe I never mentioned that I like video games. It helped a lot when Mom and Dad were fighting. Whenever they started screaming at each other, I could escape to all these digital worlds. And now, here I am, literally in a different world—a world where I'm the hero, I have powers and I'm the good guy. I may be the good guy they didn't invite out to play games, but I'm still smiling and walking, and people are still waving and smiling back because I'm the Ambassador, the one with the powers, the one who will save them all. I breathe easier remembering that. I am trying to push Mia out of my head, the one who would say anything to knock me down a peg, and then I'm forcing my smile even more because I remember that I can't even control my powers and no one knows the truth.

"Hey," Evora says, walking up. We both are standing in front of my private tent, the one Evora insisted I have, because I'm the chosen Ambassador.

"What's up," I say back, rubbing my hand through my hair, flexing a little as I do.

Her eyes are twinkling and she's looking pretty great as usual. "I can't find your sister anywhere," she grumbles.

"Yeah. I haven't seen her either." So, I lie. Not really to protect Mia, but honestly because I don't want Evora training Mia in Aveth. I want to be the only one.

She puts her hands into the air. "I give up. No more hunting for her tonight."

I shrug. "Do you really need her to learn it anyway?"

Our eyes meet. "Maybe not."

And there's my smile again. She smiles too. I don't want to look away.

"Can we talk for a moment?" she asks me.

"Yeah! For sure!" I open my tent flap, which is made from some kind of animal skin, and she ducks in. I follow her. I wish I knew she had been coming, because after we set up camp, I

literally just dumped everything out of my wooden crate looking for the shirt I like best. My tent is a disaster, but let's just
say, you should see the disaster zone that is my room at home.
I mean, I think we lost baby Zoey under a pile of clothes for a
week or two.

I'm quickly grabbing clothes off the ground (they gave me
a whole new wardrobe) and throwing them back into the crate.
I notice my red flannel at the bottom—yep, I kept my clothes,
unlike Mia—and I'm stuffing everything on top of it. I notice
the unlit candles, and I'm about to panic, because I *should* be
able to use Aveth to light them, and I'm about to attempt to do
it, but Evora does it first. I act like it's not a big deal, so I keep
cleaning and I wish I could put on my playlist or something to
help the mood. I can feel Evora watching me as I'm running
around making things look nice, and she sits down on the only
place to sit, which is the cushion where I sleep.

"Sorry about the mess."

She only smiles. And I'm done cleaning and I stand there
awkwardly because I'm not sure where to sit.

"You're cute," I hear her say, and her smile has grown.

"I get that a lot," I respond cleverly. My heart starts to
beat faster and I wonder if I should tell her she's pretty or something, but my mouth is suddenly really dry and words won't
form. She called me cute and I know I'm cute, but she actually
said it, and I'm still not saying anything.

She looks down. "I'm really glad you're here." She pauses.
"Oliver, I wanted to thank you."

"For what?" I ask, deciding to just sit on the ground. I'm
pretty close to her, but I need to leave room for the Holy Spirit
if you know what I mean.

"Everything. For coming here. For being brave. For learning Aveth. For...caring about me."

"Honestly, being here has been so awesome. I've met great
people, I got to meet... *you*."

"Life with Odynne hasn't been easy, and I've struggled
my entire life to prove to my parents that...that I could be
important too. Finding you, saving you, has been my greatest
achievement. If you could have seen the look in my father's

eyes when he first saw me after we went to the Oasis city, he was *so* proud of me. I never want that to go away." She's remembering it in her head, and there's sadness but also flickers of joy in her beautiful eyes.

"I know the feeling."

"You do?" she asks, scooting a little bit closer to me.

"Yeah, my dad got remarried, and her name is Tracy. She's cool or whatever, and they have a new baby together, Zoey. And I try to give him his space, you know? Because he has this new...uh...family to take care of, but I know what you mean. I want," I swallow, and I don't know why I'm feeling so sappy about all of this, "I want him to be proud of me."

"Well, I'm proud of you."

I smile.

She reaches out and grabs my hands. My heart is racing. She squeezes them and I squeeze back.

"Look, Evora, I'm gonna do *whatever* I can to help you close that portal. And your dad is going to know for sure that it's only because Evora, the best daughter, made it happen." I look around. "I mean, I don't see Odynne anywhere trying to close portals, do you?"

"Maybe she's hiding with Mia."

We both giggle, and we're still holding hands. I notice some loose hair has fallen in front of her eyes, and I slowly reach out to her face and gently move it away from her eyes and tuck it behind her ears, you know, like they do in movies. Now my hand is on the back of her head, and I want to kiss her, and woah, suddenly Courtney's face flashes before my eyes. I try not to let my eyes widen, but I suddenly wonder what she's doing, and I think about how mad she would be if she found out I kissed another girl. We haven't even broken up, and true, I can't exactly do that because I'm a little busy at the moment trying to be a hero in another world. But still, I've had exes cheat on me before and I hated the feeling, and I wouldn't want to do that to Courtney. Not again. Okay, yeah, there was this one girl, Emily, at the beginning of freshmen year. I didn't kiss her or anything, well, maybe we did kiss, like once. And Courtney never found out, and true, she wouldn't find out about Evora either. Now I'm remembering the first time I kissed Courtney, in the backseat of her sister's car at Taco Bell when she was running in to grab our food because the drive-through guy got our order wrong, and now I realize I'm just staring at Evora, holding the back of her head.

Suddenly, there's screaming and yelling and the sounds of swords clashing. We both jump up because soldiers are slashing their way into my tent, and they're on the ground unconscious now. I'm following Evora out into the night and all of this is happening really quickly. There's fire everywhere and soldiers are charging into the camp from all around us over the rocky dunes, but we aren't ready for them. I thought we had scouts on the lookout, but they stink at their job. Our soldiers are trying to fight them all off, but we're being overwhelmed. Evora is shouting commands, but I can't even hear her. I see her using Aveth to shoot more fire at the attackers, but I realize the initial fire that is burning down our camp couldn't have been Aveth. Why would we burn down our own camp? Only Evora can use Aveth, besides me, well kind of, so the attackers are burning down our camp, and we have to fight!

"We're under attack! Soldiers! To arms!" Evora is shouting. At the same time, she's holding off like eight soldiers with Aveth, and they're putting up their hands and covering their eyes from the brightness of the flames.

I notice a lot of our horses are running away from the fire and everything is in chaos. I wonder where Jai is, and I'm frantically looking around for my sword they gave me, the sword I haven't yet been trained to use, and I'm kicking myself for wasting so much time hunting with Jai instead of training with Lucius. I hope he's okay. I hope Mia's okay. Mia! Where's Mia?

"Mia!" I call out. But it makes no difference. Then I feel myself being grabbed by strong arms, and I'm kicking and twisting and trying to get away. I throw my head back and it hits the guy in the face, and he drops me. We're both on the ground and I'm crawling away from him as fast as I can. But he grabs my legs. So, I'm kicking hard, like he's the ball, and I'm strong, so I get free, and I try to swing my sword, but I realize I'm not even holding it, because I dropped it when he grabbed me. And I'm trying to find it, but he's clutching at me again. He's so strong, and he's trying to tie me up. I have a mouth full of sand now, and I'm trying to call out, but I can't. I see Jai fighting two guys at once, but he doesn't see me, and

I'm trying to call his name, but the guy flips me over, and is sitting on top of me now. I look into his eyes, and honestly, the guy looks just as scared as I do. He doesn't look evil or angry; he just looks frantic and terrified. I'm twisting and moving, and trying to throw him off of me, when suddenly someone has plowed into him, and they're both on the ground fighting and throwing punches and elbows. It was Linnetia and I'm so glad she came. The back of my head hurts and I think I scratched my leg or something, and I stagger to stand. The fires are growing and I don't see Evora anymore, and I'm trying to get my bearings, trying to figure out where in the camp I'm at, or where Mia could be, because I know she's practically helpless and I'd never forgive myself if anything happened to her.

"Mia!" I shout as a horse stampedes by me, nearing knocking me over, and I think it's Horse. "Mia!" I shout again, looking everywhere. But the smoke is getting so thick I start to cough, and I can't really see much. I grab a random sword on the ground and I hold it up in front of me for protection. I need to use Aveth, and I know I need to use Aveth, and now is the time to use Aveth, but I'm shaking because this is so much more real than a video game. In video games you can respawn if you die, and I'm guessing that isn't going to happen here, because I'm seeing some dead bodies as I stagger through the smoke and screams and whining horses and intense heat. I wish the Shadim would come and save us. I wish the Emperor would appear and blast away these attackers with whatever power Emperors of different worlds might have.

And I'm realizing Mia is crazy to think that *these* could be the good guys. These guys who ambush us at night, burn our camp and ruin my romantic moment with Evora. "Mia!" I shout again, and I think I see something in the smoke, so I start to stagger toward it. It looks like two people and two horses just standing there, and they aren't running or moving or fighting. Wait, is that three people? I can't tell, and two soldiers are suddenly brawling right in front of me, and they fall before my feet. They're punching and slashing, and I jump over them and start to move faster, because I think I recognize the third person.

It's Mia.

"Mia!"

And our eyes meet, and she looks terrified.

She's tied up. She can't move. Two warriors in black stand on either side of her. They lift her up and place her on a horse. One warrior gets on with her, the other mounts a different horse. And they start to gallop away.

"Stop!" I shout, terror slamming into my body.

They don't stop.

And I feel heat behind me, because Evora appears, shooting Aveth at them, intense waves of fiery heat.

"Oliver! Aveth!" She commands. She starts to run after them, and I'm following.

"Oliver! Do it!"

And I'm trying, and they have Mia, and I have to save her. I'm still trying, and I'm looking at the moon, because the suns are gone, and nothing is happening. I'm praying and I'm trying again and I'm pleading, and I'm thinking and I'm desperate. Nothing is happening and the horses are getting farther and farther away. Evora has stopped running now and she turns around and looks at me with this face so full of disappointment and confusion.

"What's the matter with you?" she shouts at me. I've never heard her so angry or intense. Her eyes are fiery too and she's fuming and I'm slightly terrified of her. "Why didn't you use Aveth?" She's right up in my face now, and I'm guessing she doesn't want me to kiss her at the moment.

I sigh and look down. "Because...I can't."

"What do you mean you *can't?* You've done it *before!*" She's insanely frustrated and I understand why. I mean, I've been lying to her, to everyone for days, but now's not the time for this because they have Mia and we have to get her back, but the horses have disappeared now and Mia with them.

"We have to follow them!" I shout, running in their direction.

"You'll never catch them now. Maybe if you had used *Aveth* it would have been enough firepower to spook the horses." And she's storming away from me.

"Wait!" I call out. "We have to go after her!"

But Evora isn't turning around.

"Evora!"

What have I done?

I'm looking now, and the attackers are fleeing from the burning camp in all directions. Why stay? They have what they came for.

I turn around and look down, and there's Pluto, howling sadly into the night. And there's Mia's journal on the ground next to the shaking dog. I bend down and grab it. I open it to the first page. I've never opened it before. There's a paragraph written from Dad. The bottom line stands out to me:

"You can tell who follows the one true king by how they treat someone else. Love, Dad."

The one true king?

I look up again and at the burning camp. Pluto is still howling behind me. I fall to my knees, clutching Mia's journal in my hand.

What have I done?

Chapter 13
Study Questions

1. Oliver wears a mask; he puts on fake smiles and presents himself to be more than he is. Do you ever wear a mask? Do you think other people at school wear masks too? Why is this a bad idea? What would it take for everyone to put their masks away and present themselves as who they really are?

2. Oliver plays video games to escape. Have you ever done this? Maybe you do something else to escape your pain—what do you use? Is this good or bad? What are some healthy ways to cope with the difficult things you face?

3. Oliver has tried really hard to keep his secret. Do you have a big secret you've never told anyone? How has this affected you?

4. When things get really bad, Oliver cares about Mia. What do you think adversity brings people together? Why can't people care as much during the good times too?

5. Read Hebrews 10:36-38. When things aren't going well, it can be easy to give up—yet God calls us to endure. Send up a prayer to God to give you peace if you find yourself going through something challenging today.

Chapter 14:
So, I'm a Hostage and It's So Not Cool
Mia

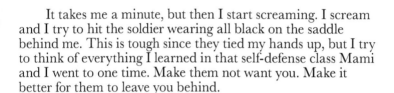

It takes me a minute, but then I start screaming. I scream and I try to hit the soldier wearing all black on the saddle behind me. This is tough since they tied my hands up, but I try to think of everything I learned in that self-defense class Mami and I went to one time. Make them not want you. Make it better for them to leave you behind.

So, I scream, "Help!" and I even scream, "Oliver!" But the two soldiers just keep riding, and we are joined by other people on horseback also in black. At one point I do succeed in smashing the back of my head against the front of the other person's head, which instantly gives me a pounding headache, but I hear her grunt. She gets really angry after that and ties a piece of black cloth around my head so that I can't scream anymore.

That doesn't stop me from trying.

Because I'm terrified.

I can't believe I've been kidnapped.

I can't believe that, for one second, I thought these were the good guys.

Moments of my life flash before my eyes. I think about when the four of us were all together. I think about the move to Cedar Park. I think about my fun times with Lito and Lita. I even think about that one moment when Zoey was born when I thought, wow, I actually get to be a big sister. And I wonder if I'll ever see any of them again. Or, is this it for me? Where are they taking me? What are they going to do to me? I know I said that Steve wasn't trying to kill Oliver and me, but that was a whole lot easier to imagine from the safety of the Rukin camp with Oliver and the dog and people who are nice to me and don't tie me up or gag me.

Steve isn't here anyway, as far as I can tell. Both of the women who were with him last time are here, though, so I think this is probably his group. Plus, it's dark, and that makes it a whole lot harder to identify anyone.

I don't know how long we ride this way, but it seems to be several hours. The night gets darker, and it begins to get colder and colder. I know what this probably means. They're taking me to Kaalinon.

Sure enough, what feels like hours and hours later, my hands feel like they're frozen together and I'm shivering all over, and we go through what looks like a valley between two mountains. At the other end of it are soldiers all dressed in white carrying a flag with a snowflake. My eyes widen. I can't let them take me across the border. Oliver and Evora will never find me in enemy territory. Even the army from Rukin will have a hard time getting into this kingdom. A tall man in white steps forward. Did I mention that there are a bunch of weapons pointed at us?

"Who goes there?" he asks.

The woman to my left raises her hands in the air and shouts, "The farmer waits for his land to yield crops, the autumn, and the spring rains."

The man pauses, then replies, "And so we wait for the return of the Prince."

There is an understanding between everyone, like an inside joke that I am not a part of. But the sea of people parts, and we are let through.

A group of people come to tend the horses, I guess. These horses were running fast for a long time and look pretty tired. "We'll give you ours," a woman assures the person behind me. How nice of them.

I am pulled off of the horse and my legs feel stiff and rubbery all at the same time. I fall to the cold ground, trying to catch myself while my hands are still tied. I shove my tangled hair out of my face.

Then, I realize that, for a second, nobody is looking at me. The woman I was on the horse with is putting on a heavy white coat. The woman who was next to us is transferring items from her horse to a new one. Everybody is busy.

It's now or never.

Slowly, I get to my knees. Still, no one is paying attention. I spot a clearing up ahead. If I can just get back into Rukin, I might have a chance. I get one foot underneath me, then the other. I take a deep breath and BOLT.

"Hey, stop her!" someone shouts immediately. But I shove past one guy who tries to grab me and twirl past another from the other side. I try to channel my inner football star, but with higher stakes because I'm not running for a touchdown but for my life.

And just like a lot of football stars, I am tackled to the ground way before I reach my destination. It is a big burly man with bright red hair and a handlebar mustache. "Got her," he says as he pulls me up. I am so frustrated; I feel tears welling at the corners of my eyes.

A crowd gathers around us as the man pulls me to my feet. I'm still cold and shaking and super scared. The guy has a grip on my arm, and it hurts, and everyone is looking at me. I feel so alone, and I hate feeling alone.

Then, a small-framed soldier with straight dark hair and narrow eyes steps forward. "Really, Bedic, she's just a child, you can let her go."

Bedic, the guy holding me, huffs and releases my arm. "Well, she was running away, Edie. What was I supposed to do?"

Edie sees that I'm shivering and sniffling and she pulls me away from Bedic. "You poor thing," she says. I see some wrinkles around her eyes, but her face looks warm, and she reminds me a little of my mom. I want to trust her, but I'm still not sure I should. "Here, take this," she tells me. She takes off her white coat and places it around my shoulders. The warmth instantly starts to envelope me, but I'm still shivering.

The woman who had been on the horse with me rushes up. She has changed now and blends in with the rest of the soldiers, but I still recognize her as one of the soldiers who attacked us back in Rukin. We have the same color skin tone, but she's way taller and stronger and more intimidating than I could ever be. Also, she's got a bruise on her cheek from when I smacked her with my head. You asked for it, lady. "Sorry about that," she says gruffly, reaching for my arm.

"Is all this really necessary?" Edie asks, pointing to my hands and mouth.

"We can't trust her. She's been traveling with Princess Evora for weeks. Also, she wouldn't shut up."

"But, Jayde, isn't she the Ambassador?" Edie questions. I can tell she's cold without her jacket, but I'm still shivering and not really in a position to give it back. "I've heard stories..." Other people mumble around us.

I-guess-her-name-is-Jayde realizes that everyone is staring at us. "Where is Rydan?" she snaps.

Bedic steps forward. "He's in a camp about an hour north of here. I'll take you there. We best get going soon. A snowstorm is coming."

No, no, no, no, no. I can't go *farther* into Kaalinon. I back up frantically, but Jayde is still there and she looks so angry. The eye above the cheek where I hit her is red and puffy, and I'm worried she'll want revenge, and I can do nothing about it, and where is Oliver?

Maybe he's not coming for me.

"At least the gag?" Edie says softly.

"Fine." Jayde grunts and yanks it off roughly. I cough and sputter. It's like my lips have fallen asleep. "You scream again, and it goes right back on," she snaps at me.

I nod, still coughing a bit. But, if I spot a rescue squad, you bet I'm screaming my lungs out.

That's the thing, though. Nobody knows where I am. All my hope of rescue or escape (I'm a 21st century lady, after all) begin to dwindle. I'm hungry. I'm thirsty. I'm tired. I'm still very cold.

Edie touches my arm softly and smiles. "Stay strong, dear. You're braver than you know."

I wish that was true, lady. I'm not feeling very strong right about now.

I end up on another horse, and we ride away as the snow starts softly falling. That's when those welled-up tears in my eyes spill over. They spill down my face and I feel them making little frozen trails and pooling at the neck of the coat.

Awhile later, I've lost track of time, and it's snowing pretty hard. I see a couple log cabins up ahead. The idea of being *inside* is enough to make me almost happy. As I'm taken off the horse, I begin to move toward the cabin, but instead, Jayde yanks me toward what is clearly a stable. "Hey!" I shout at her.

"You're a stranger, and I don't trust you," Jayde says matter-of-factly.

I keep pulling against her, but she is so annoyingly strong. "Jayde, come on." It's the dark-skinned soldier who was riding next to us.

"We don't know if they taught it to her. You wanna stick her in a wooden cabin with us, Afya?"

Aveth. I'm wishing I *had* learned it right about now.

"We're all cold," Afya argues. "She's just a kid."

"*You're* just a kid," Jayde snaps.

I look at Afya again. Sure enough, she can't be too many years older than me.

"Then let Rydan decide."

Jayde sighs. "You only say that because you know he'll side with you."

But she brings me inside and I find out that Steve, the guy with the scar, is actually Rydan. "Of course," I sigh. The guy is obsessed with us.

Rydan is sitting on a stool by the fire. He is wearing pieces of Kaalinon's uniform which is basically a white Under Armor type shirt and what look like ski pants. He stands up quickly as we enter the cabin.

He looks from me to Afya. "What about the boy? I thought we decided..."

"We tried, but he got away again. We almost couldn't even get her. There's a lot of them, and they're strong."

"I'm right here," I say through chattering teeth. "You can

123

stop talking about me in the third person."

Rydan runs his hands through his hair the same way Oliver does sometimes, and I realize his arm is out of the sling. "Bring her by the fire," he directs. I see Jayde glare at Afya, but she does what he commands.

I have half a mind to remind him to stop ignoring me but one: he looks upset that he didn't get Oliver also, and two: a warm fire looks pretty inviting right about now.

There are furs on the wooden floor by the fireplace and I gag a little bit, but sit on them anyway because, if nothing else, they are very cozy looking. Rydan sits back on the stool in front of me. He's towering over me, and if he's trying to intimidate me, it's working, but I scowl back anyway.

"What's your name?"

I raise an eyebrow. "Nope."

"And, Nope, was it you who came through the portal in Canterbor?"

"No, nope isn't my name…"

"Then why did you say…"

"…I was just being defiant…"

"…that it was?"

We were both talking at the same time and we both stop at the same time too. Rydan looks angrier now. Bedic enters the cabin, and waves to us both happily before heading to another room.

These people are so strange.

"What is your real name?"

"How about you untie me first?" I reply, holding up my hands.

"Not a chance."

"Then you're not getting anything out of me." I try to cross my arms and realize halfway through the attempt that this is impossible and I look really stupid while trying.

Rydan does succeed in folding his arms and raises an eyebrow, too. "You are not in a position to be making demands."

"Then why don't you just kill me?" I say. Why did I say that? Please don't kill me.

Bedic returns with a bowl of some broth that smells really good and a glass of water. He hands it to me kindly. Isn't this the same scary dude who tackled me a couple hours ago?

I sniff it suspiciously. "Is this vegetarian?" Or is it the guts of the animal skin I'm sitting on?

Rydan rolls his eyes. "It's vegetable soup."

Okay, good. What? I can't give up all my principles. I raise the spoon to my lips, then pause. "Is this poisoned?"

Bedic laughs out loud this time while Rydan grabs the spoon from me and takes a bite of it himself. "Satisfied, your Highness?"

I start eating. It's delicious. Rydan keeps asking me questions, and, yeah, I'm weak, and the food is good, and the water is refreshing. He doesn't look so scary anymore, and I tell him that my name is Mia and my brother is named Oliver, and, yes, we both came through the portal at the same time.

"This is unheard of," Rydan says softly.

Rydan gets up to say something to the other people in the room, and something about the way he's talking reminds me of Evora, but his voice is getting farther and farther away. I feel all warm and toasty even though I'm still a little scared, but the furs are so soft, and I'll lay my head down for just a second...

I wake up to bright sunshine streaming in through a window. Both suns are up in the middle of the sky. How long was I asleep? I sit up and my head immediately starts throbbing. I feel like I've been hit by a bus. I'm still on the floor where I was last night. Afya sits lazily on a wooden chair and sits up immediately once she sees my eyes open. "Good afternoon, Ambassador," she says a bit shyly. She's looking at me the way I looked at Tom Holland when I ran into him at the airport after visiting my dad.

I groan and lay back down. "Did you guys drug me?" I ask. My mind feels sluggish. I was sick with the flu last school year and it felt kind of like this.

"You're just tired from our trek yesterday. I'll get Rydan."

She leaves me alone and I look at my untied hands and the door. My heart races. Then I look beyond the door, through the window, and see a lot of freshly fallen snow. And I realize that leaving this cabin could be a worse choice than staying in it. Especially without supplies. Especially alone.

So, instead, I groan and place my hands over my eyes. I wonder what Oliver is doing right now? Is he glad to be rid of me? Are they naming him the true Ambassador yet? Has he forgotten about me already?

Rydan appears and sits on the stool again. "How are you faring, Mia?"

"Like I got hit by a...Horn Terror."

"Listen," he says as he leans forward. "It's not my intention to hurt you. I just want to talk."

I mean, wasn't I wanting a conversation with the bad guys just a few days ago? Be careful what you wish for, Mia. "So, let's talk then." I sit up slowly.

He bites his lip and thinks for a moment. "Princess Evora has been lying to you."

"Lying how?"

"She's likely told you whatever you needed to hear in order to convince you that the Emperor is just. He isn't. He is our oppressor. Long ago, he usurped the throne from the Prince..."

"Aha!" I exclaim louder than I meant to, while pointing a finger. "So, you admit, you are followers of the Dark Prince and trying to resurrect him and other evil stuff that bad guys do."

"He is not...well, I suppose...He doesn't go by the Dark Prince, first of all."

"That's what you want me to think!"

"Why would an evil person put 'dark' at the beginning of their title? Isn't that rather obvious?"

He's got me there. "Okay, what do you call him?"

"His name. Prince Kiran." Rydan says it with a sort of reverence that reminds me of when Evora mentions the Emperor. "He is the one who has promised to save Elior, not harm it. He

126

is part of the Sovereignty. He ruled Elior before the Emperor did."

My brain is too muddled for this confusing conversation. Plus, there's too much to process.

"The thing you did. Ruach." I gesture to his hands. I see the burn scars again on his forearms. I wonder if he got them because of Aveth.

"Anyone with faith in the Prince can do it. I can show you, if you'd like."

"No way, José," I snap. I have my hands full with Evora.

He sends a pulse of air into the fireplace and it somehow extinguishes the fire. Maybe science works differently here? "What can I say to convince you?"

"I don't know, man, but you shouldn't have kidnapped me for starters." I shrug. My head is feeling worse and worse and now I'm getting kind of nauseated and I'm so done with this conversation.

He answers shortly, "Look, I'm not trying to hurt you, but I needed to talk to you and it was the only thing I could think of. I need your help."

"My help to do what?"

"To defeat the Emperor."

I look at him, eyes wide. "Are you kidding me? I'm just a kid!"

"What does Evora want you to do?"

"Huh?"

"What does Evora want you to do?" he asks bitingly. It makes me a little nervous.

"We're supposed to close the portal in Kaalinon." Why did I tell him? I don't know. Maybe a little part of me wants to join the rebellion. To fight for the oppressed. If what he says is the truth. There are a lot of ifs in this situation.

"You, specifically?"

"My brother and me. It's why she's teaching us Aveth."

I can practically see wheels turning behind his eyes.

"Afya! Jayde! Come here!" he calls. "We need to talk," Rydan tells them as he hurries them outside to the other building.

I'm left alone with Bedic for a while, and I think I might have a fever. What I wouldn't give for some of my Mami's soup right about now.

Some days go by and I guess everyone realizes that I'm not looking so good. They stop interrogating me. I get to the point where I won't move from my spot by the fire and any mention of food makes me want to throw up. I can hear Rydan, Afya and Bedic and even Jayde whispering in concern for my well-being. They're my captors, and super scary, but also don't actually want me to die, and I feel too yucky to process this right now. I wish I had my journal. I hope someone picked it up back at the Rukin camp.

And then, it hits me. My backpack. My backpack! My backpack is full of my antidepressants that I have been taking daily even here in Elior. That's what's going on. I haven't taken them since I got taken from the camp.

"I need my backpack," I whisper to Afya, the person closest to me.

"Your backpack?"

"It has medicine in it. I need to take it," I tell her.

She seems to understand what I mean and jumps up to talk to the others.

A few minutes later, Bedic runs in with my backpack. "I forgot I put this in our traveling packs."

He begins to hand it to me, but Rydan stops him. "What if she has a weapon?"

"I don't," I tell him quickly. I hadn't even thought of that.

Miraculously, he believes me. Bedic hands me my backpack and I take my medication. It doesn't kick in right away, I know it won't, but my head is already starting to feel a little better. When it clears, maybe I can ask them some of *my* questions. Like why I'm tempted to believe their story about the Dark Prince. Why they didn't try to kill me. Maybe I can ask if they know who the true king is.

Chapter 14
Study Questions

1. Have you ever been in a scary situation? How did you feel? What did you do?

2. Mia isn't sure whether to believe what Rydan tells her, or if she should believe Evora. At this point in the story, who do you believe? What evidence do you have that either Aveth or Ruach is good or bad?

3. Read Matthew 25:31-40 and compare it to Hebrews 13:1-2. What do these verses tell us about how to treat others?

4. Read Hebrews 12:14 and say a prayer asking God to give you the strength to show kindness to everyone, even your enemies.

Chapter 15:
So, Look At Me Now, Dad
Oliver

The snow is coming down so hard it's difficult to keep my eyes open. I feel like a popsicle; every part of me is cold. I'm literally shaking. We crouch behind a large rock and wait for Vesper to peek above the boulder to get a better look. We watch as her purple eyes widen.

"What is it?" Evora asks.

"There are more troops than we thought."

"What do we do?" Evora questions again.

"We do what they least expect."

I look at Lucius and Evora and they are still staring at Vesper.

"Which is?" I stutter.

Vesper opens up her hand and the warmth of Aveth appears, casting a glow on her eyes and face. "We rush in."

Evora nods and draws Aveth into the palm of her hand. Lucius readies his weapon. I look down and open my hand. A red flame appears, and I nod to all of them.

We charge down into the valley of enemy soldiers.

Okay, okay, I know this is really confusing. Who is Vesper? How am I using Aveth? Why are we charging against an entire army with only four people? What about Mia? Well, just calm down and let me back up a little bit and explain. A lot has happened, okay? There isn't a lot of time left, so stay with me.

Let's back up to the night that Mia got captured. I am kneeling there dramatically if you remember, holding Mia's journal, listening to Evora shout to the Rukin soldiers to sal-

131

vage any bits of the camp they could and that they needed to move, now. I remember following her, telling her we have to go after Mia, and she is literally ignoring me, definitely in commander mode. She finally stops and turns around and gives me the most terrifying look I've ever seen, so I know to drop it at the moment. I go back to my tent and grab my stuff; luckily my tent hasn't been burned down. I am really irritated with myself for a lot of little reasons. Number one, I shouldn't have pretended to know how to use Aveth. Maybe if I had been truthful and gotten some more training, Mia would be standing here next to me, annoying me as always. Number two, I definitely should have trained with Lucius so I wasn't worthless with a sword. And number three, I should have kissed Evora when I had the chance, because I'm thinking that ship has sailed.

Eventually I'm packed up again, and we're on the move. We lost some supplies, horses, and soldiers during the attack. But Horse? Still kicking it. In fact, I'm riding him right now, and Pluto won't leave my side. I guess I'm the next best thing to Mia, even though I've gotta admit, I would have guessed she would have preferred Linnetia to me. Also, this ride through the northern deserts of Rukin at night is rough because I'm feeling even more guilty that we aren't going after Mia. But no one is currently talking to me and I have no idea where Jai and Linnetia are. My mind keeps spinning. I'm feeling totally helpless.

Lucius's voice catches me off guard, and he's suddenly riding beside me. "I'm sorry about Mia," he says sadly.

"Yeah. Some Ambassador I am."

"You should have been honest about Aveth, Oliver."

"I know. I'm sorry."

Lucius doesn't look at me; he's focusing on the trek ahead. "Don't think that Evora isn't doing anything for Mia. After she mobilized the troops, she immediately sent scouts to track the soldiers that took her. We believe they transported Mia across the border and into Kaalinon behind enemy lines, which will mean she'll be difficult to reach. Evora is in communication with King Jethil about the situation. Things are complicated. She believes we're going to need the Emperor's help with this."

My eyes widen. "What do you mean? What is he going to do?"

"I guess we'll see. I know you're *both* important to Elior, and more than that, I know that Evora and Mia are friends. We're all worried about her."

"What do you think they'll do to her?" I ask, swallowing nervously.

He puts his hand on my shoulder. "We're going to get her back."

"Lucius. What will they do to her?" I press.

He sighs heavily. "I don't know." Our eyes meet.

I'm afraid he doesn't want to tell me the truth: that they will kill her.

We continue on in silence, and I want to cry. I feel so miserable about everything. I have been such a jerk to her, and yeah, she annoys me a lot, and we don't see things the same way, but a lot of that isn't even our fault. It's because of our parents, and living far away from each other, and a bunch of other stupid things that don't really seem to matter anymore.

I don't know how long we ride, but we eventually stop for the night. Evora tells everyone we aren't staying long and to just plan to get a few hours of sleep. Most people don't even set up tents; they simply make fires and sleep next to them for warmth.

I'm camped near Jai and a couple other guys around a fire and they've been really supportive, trying to cheer me up about Mia. After a while, I hear everyone dozing off, but I just can't seem to fall asleep. My mind won't stop racing. How are we going to get Mia back? Will Evora ever stop being mad at me? Will I ever get home? How am I going to use Aveth? How am I going to close the portal? Are we going to die? I just can't sleep. I look over at my bag and grab it, inching closer to the fire so I can see better. I find Mia's journal and open it, leafing past the first page and Dad's note. I realize he never gave me anything like this before. Whatever. I'm not gonna trip about it.

I flip toward the middle, because I don't care what Mia has written before we came here. The first things I notice are a bunch of pictures of me looking like a pig. I'm not impressed. There's also a dumb drawing of me trying to fight off the Horn Terror and some random paragraphs here and there, but I don't want to really snoop into her mind too much, so I don't read those too closely. But then, something catches my eye. It's a list. It's labeled "The Dark Prince" and there are several words underneath it: Unjust. Selfish. Cruel. Terrifying. There are a bunch of other words too that are pretty bad and reading them makes me even more nervous for Mia because the people who follow this lunatic have captured her. Like, I never understand in movies or video games why these psychopaths are always trying to resurrect their evil gods or monsters or whatever. Then I see she wrote "The One True King???" And there is nothing underneath it. It seems she's just as confused about everything as I am.

I don't remember falling asleep, but I guess I do, because I'm dreaming of a giant frozen gate, and there are hundreds of ice-covered Horn Terrors with axes and swords and red eyes and Mia is chained to the gate. Then the gate smashes open and Mia gets buried beneath mounds of ice and snow and the Dark Prince emerges from the evil portal, and he's like 40 feet tall. His thousands of ice soldiers come with him, and all of them are chasing me and I can't get away. I try to use Aveth to fight them off, but I don't know how. Everyone from San Diego Academy is there and they are laughing at me, and I don't know how they got here, and Courtney is kissing Rodrigo. Now the Dark Prince is getting closer and closer to me, and I can't see his face, but he's calling my name, and he has a giant axe and he wants to kill me. And the worst part of all is I'm just in my boxers and I can't find my clothes. And now Evora is kissing Rodrigo too and then I wake up shaking and shivering. The fire has died and I'm sweating and I hate dreams and I hate the Dark Prince and all of this garbage and I want all of this to be over.

After a quick breakfast of questionably rotten bread, we are traveling again. I haven't seen Evora since she gave me that scary look, and I'm in a terrible mood, even though Jai has tried really hard to make me laugh and get my mind off of stuff. Ralik rides near me a lot of the way, and when Jai isn't paying attention, I decide to talk to him because I guess it's the least I can do for Mia. I know she cares about him.

"You okay?" I ask.

"I miss Mia," Ralik responds sadly.

"Lucius says we're gonna get her back."

"I just hope she's okay."

I sigh. "Me too."

Ralik smiles at me, and I try to smile back, but Jai is heading to me now, so I look away from Ralik and move Horse over to where Jai is. Pluto is asleep with me on the saddle. I don't know how she fits, or how she is comfortable, but the mutt is totally exhausted.

"Hey, Evora is asking for you." Jai looks at me with a serious expression.

"She is?"

"Yeah. She's riding in the rear. She wants you to hang back."

"Okay." I'm totally nervous now.

He slaps my back. "You'll be alright." I told Jai the truth about my Aveth a couple hours ago, and he laughed about it, called me something I shouldn't say, and now things are fine. Why is my relationship with Evora so much more complicated?

So, I hang back and I see Evora riding gracefully on her horse. Her hair is down and it's never down, and she's even more gorgeous than before.

"You asked for me?" I say coolly, like nothing could bother me, *ever*.

"I did." She doesn't sound mad, and it actually confuses me. In fact, there's a hint of a smile there.

"Everything okay?" And I regret asking that stupid question, because clearly, I've made things worse by lying to everyone for days.

"I wanted you to know that the Emperor has promised to personally handle the Mia situation."

"What? What does that mean?"

Her smile grows. "He's sending the Shadim."

"Woah." Ever since hearing about his most elite guard, I've wanted nothing more than to meet them.

"I wanted to apologize to you, Oliver, for snapping."

I stop her immediately. "Hey, woah, no, no, no, no, *chill,*

135

I've been the jerk, and I put everyone in danger by lying about Aveth."

"Still, I should have been patient with you. You've been so nice to me, and I-"

I interrupt again, "No, you have a lot of stress to deal with. I get it. I'm the one who is sorry. And I'll do whatever it takes to truly master Aveth, no matter how long it takes. I'm not going home till I do."

"The Emperor is going to help with that too," she says, looking at me.

"Really? Wait, can you explain something? How do you communicate? Like, you don't have a cell phone or anything."

"What is a cell phone?"

"Never mind. Can you explain?"

"Aveth, of course. Just a higher level of it." She shakes her head. "First, Oliver, you must master the basics. We can get into the higher levels later."

"Can we teleport with it too?"

"One thing at a time."

"So, you talked to the Emperor?" I ask, surprised.

"No. I spoke with my father. My father communicated with him."

"Oooooh, I see, I see. Well, that's really good news, right?"

"It is. They will meet us at the border with more imperial troops. My father said that scouts have reported a large gathering of Kaalinon soldiers, ready to stop us from entering the border."

"So, we've gotta sneak across?"

"It's not that simple. A vast mountain range separates Rukin from Kaalinon. There are three mountain passes that allow easier access. The key is figuring out which pass to use."

"Will Kaalinon defend all three?"

"Probably. That actually is to our advantage. It spreads out their forces so there are less troops to deal with."

"Got it. So, a Shadim is going to train me in Aveth?"

"That's right."

"Have you ever met one?"

"No. I've wanted to my entire life." She reaches for my hand. I take it. "We're going to get through this, Oliver. Together. We're going to get Mia back, you're going to close the portal, and the Dark Prince will be stopped once and for all."

"Evora, I believe you. Most of all...I believe in us. We can do this."

She smiles again. "I really only want Elior to be safe. We suffered for too many years living in fear of the Dark Prince's return. Elior is dying and people are at war. The Emperor just wants us to live in peace."

"I'm grateful for his help."

"So am I. Oliver, I can't even begin to tell you all he's done for my family and his people." Her eyes twinkle. "Don't tell Lucius, it's a surprise. Father told me that the Emperor has his best scientists working on a cure to heal little Vyn. He does so much good for people and they don't even know about it. He doesn't care about the credit. It's the Dark Prince's goal to undermine everything he does and to bring destruction and chaos. We have to stop him."

Determination fills my heart. "We will. I promise."

She squeezes my hand again. "Come on, ride with me. Let's ride to the front. Together."

"Together," I repeat. My heart is racing again, and I think maybe things could turn out okay after all.

As we continue to ride north, the desert hills grow in size and the sand is replaced by more and more rocks. The air gets colder and more and more patches of snow are appearing on the ground beneath us. I like snow, but mostly when I'm stuffed in my snowboarding gear and we're on vacation in Colorado. Riding through this freezing air on horseback is a different story. I'm super grateful that we are prepared. I have a nice fur coat and warm pants. I do my best to keep Pluto warm too. Not because I like her at all, but because Mia does.

Eventually we find ourselves at the border between Rukin

and Kaalinon. I learn that one mountain pass is to the northwest, one is to the northeast and one is directly north of us. We stop and make camp at the base of a large ridge, the last ridge in the Kingdom of Rukin. I'm in awe. Our camp has tripled in size.

"Imperial troops," Jai smiles. We are both looking around at all the men and women dressed in gold. They have golden banners whipping in the wind with a flame stitched into the fabric—the flame of Aveth, which is the sign of the Emperor. I look at the Rukin banner with the orange sun flying beside the golden banner with the flame, and I think that with the Emperor on our side, we stand a pretty good chance.

Soon, I find myself standing in front of a very large command tent. The imperial troops set it up in anticipation of Evora's arrival. I stand there nervously with Evora and Lucius and I'm told by an imperial soldier that Pluto has to stay outside. I hand her to Linnetia who is excited to dog-sit for a while, and I try to calm my nerves. I know the Shadim wait inside, and I'm not sure what to expect. I grab Evora's hand this time; it's becoming a familiar thing. She looks at me and nods. I let go, and we step inside.

The inside of the command tent is what you'd expect to see, and what I have seen many times in video games: a basic wooden table with a red cover, wooden benches, a big map of Elior which I'm interested in seeing because I haven't seen one yet, and candles flickering with light and warmth. Standing behind the table are two very tall people, a man and a woman, wearing white and gold. They both have on white breastplates with golden flames and golden shiny capes flowing down to the ground, and speckled white and gold pants. They are both at least two heads taller than Lucius, buff, and intimidating. However, their faces are not so intimidating because they both are both smiling and looking friendly, and it's a weird sight to see.

"Come in, please come in. We're so glad you made it safely," the woman says, bringing us in and inviting us to sit on the benches. She's immediately serving us something warm and delicious to drink that's like a mix between hot chocolate and a chai latte, Tracy's favorite. The woman has dark skin, a long black braid coming down her shoulder, and wow, purple eyes. The guy looks like a giant surfer from California with blonde hair, super pale skin, and broad shoulders. He has big hands and sparkling blue eyes. I immediately LOVE these two.

I lean over to Lucius. "Shadim?"

"I think so," he whispers back.

The blonde dude sits across from us. "I'm Haston, and this is Vesper."

The woman nods and sits next to him. "We're glad you're here."

"This is Princess Evora of Rukin, Ambassador Oliver and I'm Lucius, Evora's guard."

"Thank you for receiving us and for preparing camp," Evora says. She's so professional, like a lawyer or a CEO of a company or something awesome and I sit up straight because this is so formal.

"We have discovered Mia's location," Haston begins, "and after this meeting I will depart immediately with imperial troops to retrieve her."

I'm no longer scared for Mia, by the way. I'm pretty sure Haston has never been picked last for anything in his life.

Vesper continues, "Our troops will attack the central pass as a diversion—it is the least guarded and they will be forced to reroute troops while we head for the northeastern pass and cross there."

"And the portal?" Evora asks.

"After I rescue Mia, we will meet you near the portal. The frozen gate waits in a cave deep in the snowy mountains. It will also be heavily guarded. We've marked the location on the map," Haston points to the table. "With two Shadim and two Aveth users, we will be victorious."

Two? Does he mean me?

"The Dark Prince will be sealed away," Vesper adds.

"We will yield to your judgment and command," Evora responds.

"Oliver, we understand you're having trouble using Aveth?" Vesper looks at me with a smile that is full of understanding. Haston grins too.

"Yeah, unfortunately."

"That's okay." Haston adds, "I'm going to personally train you."

I sit up straighter. "I'm ready."

"Then let's begin. Right this way."

And before I know it, I'm outside the back of the tent with a giant blonde surfer guy and I want him to be my best friend more than anyone I've ever met.

"Aveth, while sometimes intimidating to yield, is the most rewarding and fulfilling thing you'll ever experience."

And I'm remembering how Odynne was afraid of it and how Lucius said it was destructive, that it takes a toll, but how it is necessary. I'm trying really hard to focus, but a little voice in me wonders if Mia is even still alive. "Sorry, Mr. Haston, before we begin . . ." I interrupt.

"Just Haston is fine, Oliver."

"Sorry. Haston." I look at him, and there is such kindness in his eyes. "What are they going to do...to Mia?"

Haston sighs heavily. "They won't kill her. Not yet. They want something from her first." He stops and thinks, and I can tell he's trying to choose his words carefully. "You need to understand something about the Dark Prince, Oliver, and I don't like talking about him, so let's just make this quick. The Dark Prince is the father of lies. They will stop at nothing to tarnish the name of the Emperor. They will work to twist her mind against him. They will spread lies about the truth of Aveth. They will attempt to turn her against you." He looks so, so sad. "It's true, we have waited for the Ambassadors to appear in order to seal the Frozen Gate, because Aveth users have tried before and failed." He looks down, and the guy looks like he just needs a hug. "The Shadim have tried and failed." He sighs again. "I have tried, and I have failed." Now he looks at me dead in the eye. "I will get you there, and you will succeed. With Mia it will be easier, but should Mia..." he stops himself and looks up, "fall, I believe your Aveth will be enough."

This is a lot to take in, and I'm very confused and I'm not sure how to understand all that I'm hearing but I'm doing my best to listen and to stay with him.

"Emperor Zohar has used the highest level of Aveth to

grant us eternal life. The Shadim chose him when others chose the Dark Prince. We have been faithful to him, and he will always be faithful to us. I suspect, if you are successful, he will use Aveth to grant you the same."

All I can do is nod, because a ton of questions I know we don't have time for are flying through my head. Does this mean Shadim can't be killed? No one can kill Haston which means he's basically the best teammate ever? I could live forever too? Would I want to live forever? There are levels of Aveth?

I decide to just ask one simple question: "So, what do I do?"

"Oliver," now he's kneeling down to look me in the eye, "people will fail you. They always will. It is the unfortunate reality of humans. We place trust and faith and hope in them, and they leave over and over again."

And I'm thinking about my dad leaving with Tracy, and my mom constantly being with Mia, and I think of the friends who have ignored me, and all the times I waited before falling asleep for Dad to come in and give me a kiss goodnight, only to hear him telling Zoey goodnight instead, and I realize Haston is right.

"Oliver, you can only depend on yourself. You *must* believe in yourself; *that* is the key to effectively using Aveth. The Emperor helped us realize we can unlock the power if we have faith in ourselves. It doesn't take much, simply faith the size of a tiny little seed. If we believe, *anything* can happen. Now, close your eyes with me, and focus."

So, I close my eyes and I think about all that I've gone through in my life, all the pain and disappointment, all those things you think about when you don't want to, all the failures and the moments you hate yourself and those nights you cry yourself to sleep or you think about how you could have done something better, and I'm saying, Oliver, it's just you now, there's no Dad, there's no Mom, there's no Mia, there's only you. Only you can seal the portal, and you have to have faith in yourself. You have to believe you can do it, and then you will. So, I forget about everyone else and everything else and I picture myself using Aveth and when I open my eyes, I'm controlling two fiery flames. I gasp and look at a smiling Haston.

"Perfect," he says.

I'm already missing Haston by the time we've left for the northeastern pass. I'm able to turn Aveth on and off quite easily now. The key is thinking about myself more than anything, and I realize, I've been pretty good at that for a long time. I remember all the times I've heard how we can do anything if we put our minds to it, and I realize everyone was right. There is potential in all of us; we only have to believe it's true.

I said my goodbyes to Jai, Ralik, and Cerise, and left Pluto with Linnetia, and everyone wished us the best of luck as we rode off like the heroes we are. I've honestly never felt better. I don't need anyone. I don't need *anyone*.

We stay close to Vesper as we ride and the air is getting thicker and colder and less easy to breathe, but it's okay because we use Aveth to stay warm. After riding for hours, we arrive at the northeastern pass.

The snow is coming down so hard it's difficult to keep my eyes open. Every part of me is cold. I'm literally shaking. We crouch behind a large rock and wait for Vesper to peek above the boulder to get a better look. We watch as her purple eyes widen.

Hey! This is where we started! Remember?

So, we charge through the enemy forces using Aveth to shield us. Let me explain. Vesper and Evora are shooting Aveth alongside us, and I'm shooting it out in front of us. Everyone is charging out of the way, because, you know, no one wants to get burned. And I can't explain it, but Vesper does something to make us go faster than anyone else—it's almost like we're a bullet shooting out of a gun, and it kind of feels like we're riding in a convertible going down the highway at 90 miles an hour, which I promise, I've never done, not even in Rodrigo's brother's car. I promise I haven't. Vesper explained earlier that the quick movement was another level of Aveth, and I'm so excited to learn all the different levels. We keep blasting through, like a shooting star, and before I know it, we aren't around any more Kaalinon soldiers, and we've left a trail of charred stone behind us.

"We did it!" Evora cries out, and we're all out of breath, except for Vesper, who looks like she's only as exhausted as someone can be after tossing a pebble.

"I hope the battle at the northern pass is going okay," Lucius adds.

"I do too. However, it served its purpose. Follow me," Vesper commands, and soon, after climbing a mountain (not as easy as it sounds), we are all hiding out in a cave facing the valley below. I'm still playing around with Aveth as we chill, and I'm wondering how Kaalinon has been able to keep the portal away from the Emperor for as long as they have against the powerful Shadim. But I don't really feel like asking more questions.

"I'm gonna go look at the view," I tell the others, and I head to the mouth of the cave. I look out at the countryside of Elior and I've gotta admit, it's really beautiful. But still, I can tell how dead the land is, it's kind of like viewing it through one of those mirrors at a fair. It looks like a foggy, sickly haze covers everything, especially from up here.

"I'm going to save this land," I whisper under my breath. "The Dark Prince will not rise, not with me here. I can do it. I can stop him." A flame of Aveth appears in my hand. "Look at me now, Dad. Look at me now."

Chapter 15
Study Questions

1. Is there anyone in your life that you're mad at or fighting with? Take a step back and think about it. What are your reasons for feeling this way? Are your reasons valid? A lot of times people tend to forget why they're even fighting.

2. Read Hebrews 5:7. What did Jesus do when He experienced trouble?

3. Oliver begins to show Ralik some kindness. What changed?

4. How do you know if someone is good or bad? How can you tell?

5. Do you face fear a lot? There are a lot of scary things in this world, but God makes us a very special promise. Read Hebrews 13:5-6. What does God promise? How do we know He'll keep His promise? Read Hebrews 6:13-15. God has done it before, and He'll do it again for you.

Chapter 16:
So, I Don't Know What Side I'm On
Mia

"What is it like where you are from?" Afya asks me.

We are lounging on a dusty old couch in one of the rooms of the log cabin.

I know, I know, when did I get all buddy-buddy with the bad guys? I wouldn't say we're best friends, but I'm feeling much better now that the medicine has kicked in, even if I'm still weak, and I found out Afya is seventeen, and she's actually pretty cool. Her hair is in long box braids that fade into a copper color. She's fascinated with my purple hair. I told her it's not my natural color and Afya told me that one time she dyed her hair green to match the color of Canterbor. Afya is kind of awkward around me like I'm a celebrity and not a captive. It's kind of awesome.

"Boring," I tell her. "We just go to school and go home. I live with my mom and it's just the two of us."

"Isn't the other Ambassador your brother?"

"It's complicated," I sigh.

"I understand," she nods. "Queen Naru of Canterbor is my cousin. I have a large family with lots of drama."

"Is everyone else in this cabin from Canterbor?"

Afya looks in the direction of the kitchen where I smell some sort of breakfast cooking. These kidnappers are even accommodating my dietary preferences. I don't know what to believe anymore.

"Bedic is from Kaalinon. This is the first time I've met him. Rydan and Jayde...well, you'll have to ask them."

Sounds juicy. "I'm not asking that jerk anything," I roll

my eyes.

Afya bites her lip. "He's not so bad once you get to know him."

"Oh, no?" I sit up. "Let's see, for starters he had you kidnap me, took me away from my brother, isn't telling me any of your plans…"

Afya sighs. "I am sorry about all of that. Rydan…he… he's a good person but that doesn't always mean he makes good decisions."

I raise an eyebrow. "He could fix a lot of it by letting me go." Is that even what I want anymore? I mean, I want to make sure Oliver is OK, but I keep getting an unsettling feeling now whenever I'm around Evora. Or, am I reading too much into nothing?

"I'll talk to him," Afya decides. "But I hope you would choose to stay anyway. We truly do need your help."

I like Afya. I don't get how someone like her could get wrapped up in a mess like this. But I like Lucius and Ralik and Cerise, too. But one side has to be wrong.

I put my hands on my forehead. Why can't anything be easy?

"And you all really believe in the Dark Prince?"

"We believe in Prince Kiran."

"Do you really think you can overthrow the Emperor or whatever? There don't seem to be very many of you." I look around the mostly empty cabin.

"There are more than you'd think," Afya assures me. "It is said that once there was an elite force that was loyal to Prince Kiran. The Malek. If we could find them perhaps we would be stronger."

Oh, great, more new words to learn. I'm about to ask for more information, but Rydan shows up and herds Afya out of the room. "I need to talk to Mia privately."

Rydan still kind of scares me, even more than Bedic and Jayde. He just seems so intense and I can't figure out what his angle is.

"How are you feeling?" he asks, and I don't know if he really cares or not.

"Better."

"Okay, here's the plan." He sits down and leans his elbows on his knees. "I've spoken to King Fronar." Rydan sees the confusion in my face and adds, "He's the king of Kaalinon. We're going to take you to his palace. We will hopefully be safe there, and we can figure out what to do next."

"You're assuming a lot here," I frown. "What if I don't want to go with you to King Frozone?"

"Look, I don't want to tie you up." It sounds like a threat.

I think back to my conversation with Afya. "And if I do want to go with you? Would you even trust me enough to let me in on the plans?"

Rydan closes his eyes for a second, maybe gathering his thoughts or deciding if I'm a flight risk. "I guess this only works if we can trust each other."

"I guess it does."

Rydan and I stare at each other, and I don't know what he's thinking, but I'm definitely thinking that I need more information before I can just decide to continue hanging out with the bad guys, or possibly the good guys, but definitely the guys my brother is against.

Rydan hasn't necessarily convinced me, but I've been thinking about it a lot the last couple days. What if they're right? What if I've been on the wrong side this whole time? Wouldn't I be crazy to not at least hear them out? Especially if it's on my own terms?

"What about my brother?"

Another touchy subject. Rydan's face clouds over. "We were willing to try and save him too. But it might be too late. He's already used Aveth. He may be in too deep. I know how Princess Evora works."

"About that…" I begin, but Rydan cuts me off.

"Just forget about him," he says harshly. "He's probably already forgotten about you. Maybe that's why there are two Ambassadors. Because the Sovereignty knew one would fall."

I don't like that answer. Sure, I want to be the real Ambassador, but...I don't know. I don't know what that really means, I guess.

Rydan stands up to leave the room. "We leave today. Give me a few moments and I'll tell you what you want to know."

As he's walking out, I say, "Rydan. Do you know who the true king is?"

He looks back and tells me. "Prince Kiran, of course."

Of course. That's what he's supposed to say.

While I wait, I decide I'll get some breakfast.

I make it to the kitchen where I find Afya and Jayde. I start chowing down in time to see Bedic rush inside out of breath. His eyes are huge as he gasps, "Shadim! RUN!"

Everyone starts to panic, and I don't know why. Rydan runs inside just as a wall of fire envelopes the cabin. The *wooden* cabin.

"We must retreat northward!" Rydan shouts.

I hurriedly grab my backpack as everyone else grabs their essential items. I don't know who Shadim is, but he or she can clearly use Aveth and isn't afraid to use it on us. "How many enemies do ya'll have?!" I exasperatedly ask Jayde, who glares at me in return.

I'm still kind of lightheaded, so Afya wraps her arm around me as we go outside. Rydan and Bedic use Ruach (I guess) to keep the fire away from us, but it has already swept the cabin and, I notice, the stable and other buildings in this little compound. I spot a tall blond guy leading the charge against us. There are a handful of soldiers with him, and their coats are orange and...oh. I see what's happening. This must be a rescue mission. They're here for me.

I have never been this popular in my life. Everyone seems to want me.

Jayde draws her sword and pushes Afya and I back. I search faces for anyone familiar. Oliver. Evora. Lucius. I don't see anybody I recognize.

"Take her! Hurry!" Rydan shouts. He's still busily trying to block the waves of fire.

Jayde grabs my arm and pulls me toward one of the horses who must have been released by Bedic once the stable caught on fire. She beckons for me to mount it, and I hesitate for just a second before doing it. We've been galloping for about a minute when we get hit by something that feels like an intense version of getting hit by a dodgeball, and extreme heat. At least, that's what it feels like for me. Jayde, who was behind me on the horse, takes the brunt of the blast of fire and we both tumble off of the horse and into a snowbank.

My leg hurts where I landed on it, and I'm gonna be sore in the morning, and my head is hurting again, and I think my hair is singed. But I'm better off than Jayde who is unconscious and there is blood, but I don't know where it's coming from. I shake her, but she doesn't respond.

Through blurry eyes I see Rydan running toward me on the right, and the blond guy on a horse galloping toward me on the left. "Mia, hurry!" Rydan shouts, reaching his hand out.

I take a couple wobbly steps in his direction when the blond guy calls out, "Mia! Oliver sent me!"

And this makes me pause. I have about two seconds to decide which way to run before they both crash into me and probably will start fighting again and maybe I lose my option to choose who I want to go with.

I realize I don't know this blond guy, but do I really know Rydan? Do I really know any of them?

I know Oliver.

Turning, I run the other direction toward the blond guy who grabs my arm and swings me onto his white horse. "Good choice," he tells me, smiling. I look back to see Rydan angrily watching as we get farther and farther away.

"I'm Haston," he tells me once we've made it a safe distance without people following.

"Mia," I share.

I'm going to skip ahead here because all I learn over the next few hours is that Haston is one of the Shadim, who work for the Emperor, and he and someone else named Vesper were called in to save me from the evil Rydan and his crew.

There is some predetermined meeting point where we stop

in the early afternoon. To me, it all just looks like snow and trees. It's sunny today, though, and the snow is reflecting the light from two suns.

We aren't waiting there for too long before I hear some horses approaching. Before I know it, Oliver, Evora, Lucius, and a woman I've never seen before come into view. Oliver shouts, "Mia!" and he jumps off of his horse and tumbles to the ground because he's super clumsy, and I jump off of my horse, and he runs to me and I run to him, and I feel his arms around me, and I'm so relieved that my eyes water up.

"I was so worried," he says softly into my ear. I think my heart melts a little.

He pulls away, but leaves his hands on my shoulders. "Are you okay?" Oliver's face darkens. "You look pale. Did they hurt you?"

"I'm okay. It wasn't that bad."

Lucius hugs me too, and tells me he's glad I'm safe.

Evora approaches me next. "Mia, I'm so glad Haston found you. The thought of you being held hostage by those terrible…" her voice trails off. "I just can't imagine."

Okay, that sounds a little dramatic, Evora, but whatever. It *was* pretty scary. At first.

And now? I glance back in the direction we came wondering if Rydan is already hot on our tail. Next I glance at our two new traveling companions. "You're Vesper?"

The woman steps forward. "I am pleased to make your acquaintance, Ambassador."

"Fancy." I accept her offered hand. She seems strong and capable.

Evora clears her throat. "Mia, do you mind if I speak to you alone for a moment?"

We step a few feet away. Evora's face hardens a bit. "I truly am glad you are safely back with us."

"Thanks. Where are the rest of the troops?"

"Still holding off Kaalinon's forces at the border, I believe. We need to get on the move soon, as I'm sure Kaalinon troops are searching for us."

"I see." I can't help but think about what Rydan said about Evora. How she would say anything to deceive me and get me on her side. Is that true? Or was he the deceiver? Should I have stayed to hear him out?

Almost as if she's reading my mind, Evora asks, "Was it the same person who tried to take you before?"

"You mean Rydan."

Evora looks at me, concern filling her eyes. "What did he say to you?"

That you're the bad guy. "Oh, nothing really…"

"Come on, Mia, you were with them for nearly a week. Did he try to get information from you? What did you tell him?"

"Gotta tell you, Evora, it seems like you're trying to get information from me right now."

"Because I was worried about you and I wanted to make sure you weren't harmed."

I hesitate before asking, "Evora, who is the true king?"

Her eyes narrow. "The Emperor, of course. Why?"

"Just wondering," I mutter. Of course she would say that. Guess I'll have to figure it out for myself.

Oliver, bless him, saves me from further interrogation when he offers to catch me up on what has been going on. Evora leaves me alone, but I can still feel her eyes burning holes in my back. Not literally.

"I'm glad you're okay. I would have been super upset if you died or something," Oliver says awkwardly.

I grin. "Aww, shucks, I didn't realize you cared."

"And look," he adds. He holds out his hand and instantly there is a flame.

Instead of being impressed, I start to get worried. My smile fades, and I lower my voice. "Listen, Oliver, I learned some things from the other side that I think you should know about." I glance at Vesper and Haston who are casually sharpening

151

their swords. "I'm not sure we have the whole story."

Oliver's face crinkles. "Don't be ridiculous, Mia. You know they would have said anything to get you to believe them."

"But what if they're right, Oliver?"

"Are you kidding me?!" he snaps. "They kidnapped you! They burned down our campsite and took you. They could have killed you. They've been hunting us since the moment we got here. And us? We *saved* you, Mia! I saved you."

My heart is racing. I whisper, "Maybe you didn't need to."

Oliver folds his arms. "Oh. I see what's happening here. They *like* you, don't they?"

"What? What are you talking about?" So what if they do?

Oliver scratches his head hard, and is turning red. "That's it! Poor Mia, super lame and weird Mia finally finds *someone* to be her friend. And you're willing to throw everything away just so they'll like you. That's pathetic. *You're* pathetic, Mia."

Okay, I'm angry now. I could slap him again. "This has nothing to do with that! You're the one who's always so worried about what people think of you. You put on whatever mask you think people want to see! I'm your sister and I don't even know who you really are!"

Oliver opens his hand and I see a flame. Aveth. "*This* is who I am, Mia. I'm better than you ever thought I was, than you ever were. Mom never saw me. Dad never saw me either. It was always about you. Do you know why I moved to California with Dad? Because Mom always loved you more!"

"What are you talking about?" He's lying. I've heard all of this from him before and he's lying. "I'm the one who's never noticed. I'm the one who Dad left behind. Who *you* left behind. You have it so easy, Oliver. Everybody likes you!"

"Yeah, finally they do. Which is why I'm not going anywhere without Evora," he assures me. "I finally have people who see me for me. So, I'm going into that cave and I'm closing that frozen gate. And I'm gonna do it with or without you. You're welcome for saving your life."

He stalks away angrily. And I don't know what to do. I

know Oliver is wrong about a lot of things, and he's so selfish, and a real jerk. But is he wrong about this? Is he wrong about Evora and Aveth and the Emperor? I don't know. I don't know if I want to stay with him and close the portal and be the hero and listen to what Evora has been telling us for weeks now. Or if I want to choose to believe Rydan and Ruach and Prince Kiran, who I know next to nothing about.

I sit down alone in the snow, wearing a white coat that someone who I thought was my enemy gave to me to keep me warm. And I don't know what to do. So, for the moment, I do nothing.

●- ●- ●- ●- ●- ●- ●- ●- ●- ●- ●- ●

Chapter 16
Study Questions

1. Have you ever gotten into a big argument with so-meone? What happened? How did it get resolved?

2. Do you think what Oliver says to Mia is fair? Do you think what Mia says to Oliver is fair? Are their emotions affecting how they are treating each other? How could this conversation go if they were both being level-headed?

3. Is it bad to argue? Is there a good way to argue? What does Hebrews 12:6 have to say about it?

4. Read 1 Peter 1:13-16. What does it mean to be holy? What does this passage tell us about how a follower of God should act?

Chapter 17:
So, We Make a Plan
Oliver

You know, just when I was actually starting to miss Mia, she has to go and say something totally irrelevant to ruin it all. She always does this. She always has to be completely ridiculous. The moment she realizes people like me more than her, she has to dye her hair or put up posters for some stupid cause or cry about a boy and hog Mom all to herself. Moving away from it all, I thought I wouldn't have to deal with it anymore. I thought Mom would beg me to stay. I thought she would try to stop Dad from taking me, but she didn't. She watched me drive away with him, and that was that, and I've hated her for it ever since, and even more, I realize I hated Mia too. Whatever. They can have each other.

I look down at the flame of Aveth in my hand as we ride toward the portal. They say it's not too far now, but that it won't be easy to get into the cave. Evora bets we're gonna be super outnumbered. But I'm not afraid. They can't stop me. No one can. I'm doing this. Even if Mia believes we're on the wrong side. I remember that Haston told me they would do anything to change her mind, even pit us against each other. Well, they did a good job. The Dark Prince is just as much of a jerk as everyone is saying he is, and his followers are no better.

Mia and I aren't talking again, and that's fine by me. I wish we could drop her off with Pluto and the others by the border of Rukin, but it's too far away now, and I have a job to do. I'm just hoping she'll stay out of my way.

The snow is coming down harder this far north and the wind is really intense. Luckily, we're prepared with lots of layers and I have a big warm blanket to wrap around myself. I cover my face so only my eyes are exposed. I look over at Evora. I just can't get over how amazing she is. For a desert girl, the snow doesn't seem to bother her at all. Her head isn't wrapped up or anything. She looks so intense and focused. She's come a long way and gone through a lot to get us here, and I want nothing more than to succeed. I want her to see how much I care about all of this; how much I care about her. Yeah. I like her. I really do. I just want to be near her, and I kind of want to tell her, but I know there are so many more important things to do, and I'm not really sure if she'll feel the same or not, and I guess I don't have time to ask if she does. Not really.

After a lot of silent riding, we reach a cave to escape the winds for the night. We've gone a long way and it feels like we crossed three or four mountains and I know the horses must be slumped. Using Aveth, Vesper creates a nice big fire and we all silently sit around it. Mia keeps trying to look at me, but I refuse to give her eye contact. I see Lucius goes by her and sits down and Vesper and Haston are talking quietly together. Evora is braiding her hair and honestly, I could watch her stare at rocks, and I'd *still* be captivated. She's so gorgeous, like, I don't know how she does it. She stands up and heads to the mouth of the cave. How could I not follow her?

"You okay?" I ask, after we're far enough away from everyone else and I know they can't hear me.

"Just thinking about everything," she breathes.

We're standing at the opening of the cave just staring out into fields of plain white snow, and I'm not gonna lie, it's totally beautiful. It stopped snowing super hard, and the stars are shining so bright, and I can't ever really see them this clearly in San Diego with all the city lights. It's cold and clear and bright and I can see Evora's face perfectly in the darkness.

"What exactly are you thinking? I want to know."

"What happens next? What happens after we close the portal? Will the Dark Prince try and find another way to get into Elior? I just don't know."

"If he does, we'll stop him," I say quickly. "There's no way I'm gonna let him hurt anyone ever again." I pause. "There's no way I'm going to let him hurt your cute self."

She looks at me and then looks down. She doesn't smile.

"Hey, are you *sure* you're okay?" I ask with concern.

"You have your life...your *real* life, in your world." She looks up at me. "After you close the portal...will you return to Canterbor, go back through the portal and...never come back?"

"What? No way! Not now, not after everything! How could you think that?"

She shrugs and wraps her arms around herself. "I'm just afraid that you'll leave and forget all about me."

"I could never forget about you." I step closer to her and I notice she's shivering a little. Maybe the cold does bother her a bit after all.

"Do you promise?" She looks up into my face with those perfect tear-filled eyes and at this point I'd promise her anything.

"I promise."

"Good." And she's leaning her head against my chest. I wonder if she can hear my heart beating faster. I wrap my arms around her and pull her in tighter for a hug.

"I'm so glad you're here," she whispers.

"Me too."

She gently pulls away and looks up at me again. Our eyes lock. I lean in.

We kiss.

What? How could I not? I mean, come on. It was the perfect moment. It feels right. It feels like it's meant to be.

The stars shine a little bit brighter by the time we return to the back of the cave. We take a moment to look at them. I'm trying hard not to smile. Okay, let's be real, I'm trying hard not to literally dance around the cave. So, instead, I look super cool and super serious and sit next to Evora and the fire.

After eating a bit of our supplies for supper, basically bread and some nuts and berries, Haston and Vesper return from doing a bit of scouting and sit closer to the fire so we can talk about the plan for tomorrow. They look very serious, and I sit up a little taller and push out my chest like the Aveth-wielding hero that I am.

"Tomorrow, we'll either have sealed the Dark Prince away once and for all, or . . ." he stops himself and looks worriedly at Vesper.

She continues for him. "Let's just make that the plan." He nods and she breathes deeply before talking again. "We've discovered that the cave to the portal has two entrances."

"Two?" Evora exclaims.

"Yes," Vespers nods. "This is to our advantage."

"How?" Lucius wonders.

Mia hasn't said anything all day. It doesn't surprise me. She literally is the most unhelpful person in the group at the moment and I'm wondering if they'll strip away her Ambassador title and replace it with "Oliver's-annoying-little-wish-she'd-go-away-sister."

"Mia, I have a very important question to ask you." Vesper's voice sharpens and now all eyes are on my sister. She shifts uncomfortably.

"Yeah?" Mia squeaks.

"Did you tell your captors that you don't know how to use Aveth? It's very important that you're truthful with me."

Mia looks like she's thinking about her answer which makes me uncomfortable. Our argument plays back in my memory, and I'm afraid *she's* going to tell Vesper she thinks she's the bad guy, bite her leg, and scurry off in the snow. Instead, Mia says, "No."

"You're absolutely sure?" Haston presses.

"Come on, Mia, tell the truth," I snap, quite helpfully in my opinion.

"Yes, I'm *sure*," Mia snaps back. "It's not like they tied me up and asked, hey, can you use Aveth?"

"What *did* they ask you?" Evora questions, and at the same time slides her hand into mine. I don't think anyone sees. I squeeze her fingers and glare at Mia.

"Yeah?" I add, once again, quite helpfully.

Mia's eyes narrow as she shifts her focus over to Evora. "I already told you everything I know."

158

Evora huffs and I squeeze again. She squeezes back and I watch Haston and Vesper look at each other and then nod.

"It should work then," Haston says to her.

"Agreed." Her focus shifts back to the rest of the group. "This is what we will do. Because there are two entrances to the cave with the portal, both entrances will be guarded. We'll need to split up. They'll know we're coming, but the fact that they don't know Mia can't use Aveth works in our favor. If we send the majority of us with Mia and attack one entrance first, it'll appear as if she's the larger threat and that entrance will appear to need more protection, hopefully drawing more guards away. This will allow Oliver to fight his way into the less guarded entrance, reach the portal, and to seal it."

"Because Mia never learned Aveth," Evora quickly adds.

I swallow uncomfortably. "I'm going alone?" I try to say like I'm not completely freaked out.

"No. I'll be with you," Haston smiles.

What a guy. I'll have the dude who can't die on my side. I'm liking my odds.

"Are you okay with this?" Vesper asks Mia. "We don't want you to be scared."

"But she can't defend herself," Lucius says.

"Then we will have to defend her," Vespers says with confidence. She looks straight at Mia. "I promise, I won't let anything happen to you. Princess Evora and Lucius will be there too."

"Are you sure about this?" Lucius asks.

"What other choice do we have? We are running out of time!" Vesper presses and I wonder if the Dark Prince might pop out of that portal right before I get the chance to seal it, and I'm suddenly considering that maybe we should leave right now.

"Can we send for more Shadim to join us with Mia?" Evora looks at Vesper.

She nods. "I will contact the Emperor with Aveth. Mia will be well protected."

"Mia, how do you feel about this?" Lucius asks her again. She sits completely still, and I wonder if she fell asleep with her eyes open. She would do something weird like that.

After a long moment of awkward silence, Mia only nods. She doesn't say a word.

"Then we have a plan," Haston confirms with confidence, and I feel like we might actually have a chance. "Get some sleep. We leave at dawn."

Mia gets up and walks to the back of the cave. She has her journal that I so kindly returned to her in her hand. I didn't have to do that. She didn't even say thanks or anything. So ungrateful.

I spend the rest of the evening just chatting with Evora, not about anything super serious. I tell her goodnight, and she kisses me on the cheek. What? Can you blame her? After all, I'm the *true* Ambassador of Elior. It was me this whole time; did you ever have any doubt? I'm feeling great about everything. I notice Mia returning from her journal time. She takes her place on her bedroll and curls over onto her side. Something in me wants to go over to her and see how she's actually feeling about everything, but I can't get my legs to walk me over there. I just don't know what I'd say. This is the reality of our relationship. We aren't close. I don't think we ever will be. But that doesn't mean I want her to die tomorrow. It doesn't mean I want something bad to happen to her. I probably should wish her luck or something. So, I stand up and move toward where she is lying. As soon as I approach, she starts "snoring" really loud. She totally isn't asleep; she just doesn't want to talk to me. Okay, whatever, Mia. I'll go talk to Lucius instead.

He's at the mouth of the cave, the same place Evora and I shared our first (and hopefully not our last) kiss. He's staring at the stars. I don't blame him. They're hard to ignore.

"You okay, Lucius?"

"Just thinking about my family."

"I bet they're thinking about you too." I smile, and then I wonder if maybe he wanted to be alone. "I'll give you some space."

"No. Please. Stay. I'd like the company."

"Okay." So, I sit beside him. I don't even know for how long. I don't even say anything to him. But sometimes you don't have to say something to someone to let them know how you feel about them. His silence says a lot. And I hear him loud and clear. It says, I'm proud of you, Oliver. And I know he is. And nothing feels better.

The fire is mostly out by the time I lay down to go to sleep. I make it bigger again with Aveth and put my head down on my makeshift pillow to get some sleep. I know Mia is awake too. I see her sitting up and readjusting to get more comfortable. Our eyes meet.

"Good luck tomorrow," she quietly says to me.

"You too," I mutter back.

Inside I wish we can say more. But sometimes words are hard. But we do our best with them anyway, and pray that somehow our best will be enough.

Chapter 17
Study Questions

1. Read 2 Peter 3:8-9. Sometimes waiting for God to make things right feels like an eternity. How do we live while waiting? Read 2 Peter 3:14-15. What can you take away from this?

2. Oliver and Mia share a quiet moment together at the end of the chapter. They have been through a lot but the fact that they are family keeps them together. Are you close with your family? How can you improve your relationships with members of your family?

3. Read 1 Peter 4:7-11. As this story is coming to an end, what does this passage tell us? How can we apply these precious words to our lives?

Chapter 18:
So, I Turn Around
Mia

"Can you remind me exactly what we're about to do here?" I ask Vesper hesitantly. There are four of us: me, Vesper, Evora, and Lucius, and we left our horses tied to a tree at the bottom of the hill. Now we're trekking up this snowy hill and I suppose the entrance to the cave is up ahead. It's pretty windy, and the cold burns my cheeks and makes my lips feel dry.

I kind of know what the plan is already, but I'm super nervous, and I haven't been able to make a decision about what side I want to be on, and I'm worried someone is going to get hurt if I don't make up my mind one way or another.

Oh, and Evora has not said *one* word to me since my fight with Oliver. She's been acting stone cold. I guess that's because she's questioning my loyalty. But I'm here, aren't I? I'm climbing up this hill, totally out of breath and nervous and without a weapon because they wouldn't give me one.

"You're with us to draw the army's attention away from Oliver and Haston. They must be waiting for us at the top of this hill." Vesper speaks to me sternly. Nobody is in a talkative mood right now. I can just feel the tension.

"Right," I say to myself. That can't be too bad. I'm not doing anything too bad. I'm not.

I'm not.

Then why do I feel so horrible?

Every step I take up this hill, it seems like some invisible force is trying to push me backward. I keep thinking, turn around, Mia, run, Mia, go back to the horses, Mia. And it is a nearly overwhelming urge, like when I was younger and I heard my parents fighting, but I kept tiptoeing toward the kitchen, and something inside me told me turn around, Mia, you shouldn't be listening, it will just hurt you, but I didn't, I kept walking. I can still hear that argument and those hateful words between them in my head right now. And even that noise isn't enough to drown out that incessant voice in my head telling me to turn around, and that twist in my gut telling me something is wrong.

"You can do this, Mia," Lucius tells me suddenly. He was walking just a couple paces behind me. I slow down so we can walk in stride.

"How do you know?" I ask nervously.

"Because I've seen you. You're brave. You were chosen to be the Ambassador for a reason."

"Yeah, chosen by who?"

Lucius looks up thoughtfully. "I'm not sure. But Someone knows your character. Someone knows that you will do the right thing even if it's not easy. All it takes is a little faith."

Something about what he says reminds me of this Bible story I learned at school a long time ago. I don't remember exactly what it says, and I don't remember exactly where in the Bible it is, but Jesus says something about having faith the size of a mustard seed. My teacher brought actual mustard seeds and they were teeny tiny even in my small hand. There was something about faith the size of a tiny seed being able to move a mountain. And that sounds pretty ridiculous as I'm climbing a tall hill that's maybe not even a mountain, and it's still way bigger than me.

I've never really thought of this story before, and I don't know why I'm thinking of it now. I've never really had faith in anything. I've been let down by everyone I've trusted. I've let down everybody, too.

I've been thinking a lot about that verse my dad wrote in my journal. About how you can find the true followers of God by their actions. And, sure, we're in Elior now, and it's a whole different place, but somehow I feel like the rules here are the same. Maybe God has a different name here, but also maybe he's still around.

And I think about the way Rydan and his group treated me when they didn't even know they could trust me. How

164

they fed me and clothed me and took care of me and treated me with respect even though I had been traveling with their enemy. And I think about the way Evora hasn't been talking to me, and how she kind of uses Oliver but he doesn't see it, and how she's clearly hiding something from us.

These thoughts keep whirling through my mind until Evora, who is at the lead, stops us all. "We are near the top of the hill. We must be prepared for a battle once we reach the top."

Oh, wow. It's really happening.

Turn around, Mia.

Go back to the horses, Mia.

I nervously tap my fingers together.

Evora, Lucius, and Vesper draw their swords. "On the count of three," Vesper whispers.

She counts one, two, THREE! We all rush around an outcropping of rock ready to fight.

And there is no one here. We are all alone at the top of a hill with a cave entrance jutting out to the left.

"Where are they?" Lucius asks. And it seems we are all wondering the same thing.

"Maybe we got here first," Evora guesses.

"How would that make any sense?" I ask. "This is Kaalinon's portal, right? Why wouldn't they be guarding it?"

"Well, they're not here," Vesper says. "Evora is right. They must not have been expecting us this quickly."

I am not satisfied with this answer, and Lucius doesn't seem to be either, but we're not the ones in charge, so our questions get shut down. Our questions happen to be important things like, "Where is the army you said would be up here?" and "Are you sure this is the right place?"

"We should split up," Vesper decides. "Lucius and I will return to the base of the hill where we can stand guard against any forces that may show up. Mia and Evora will go into the cave."

"I don't leave Evora," Lucius says firmly.

"We aren't leaving her. She'll be perfectly fine. Nobody is here," Vesper snaps.

Lucius is unconvinced, but Evora nods her head at him. "Mia and I will be fine. Won't we, Mia?"

I don't feel like answering her. Ignoring can go two ways, buddy.

Eventually Lucius sullenly agrees. He squeezes my hand, tells Evora to be careful, and he and Vesper head back down the hill. Evora and I stand in front of the dark cave. Evora lights the torch using Aveth and we step into the mouth of the cave to get out of the wind.

She hands me the torch. "You go first. I'll follow behind you."

"Why do I have to go first? I don't have a weapon." Turn around, Mia. Go back to the horses, Mia.

"You have the light." Evora points to the torch. "I have the sword." She draws her sword.

"How about you give me the sword and use your hand as light."

Evora rolls her eyes at me. "Just walk."

My heart beating rapidly. I begin to slowly walk deeper into the cave. Pretty soon all light except for the one I'm carrying is gone. "How much farther?"

"I don't know. Keep walking."

I keep walking. Turn around, Mia. Go back to the horses, Mia.

I notice this cave is pretty shallow and doesn't have any caverns that branch off from this main one. I'm only walking for a few minutes when my way becomes blocked by a stone wall. I touch it. "This is the back of the cave. What now?" I ask.

TURN AROUND, MIA!

I turn around just in time to see Evora plunge her sword right at my stomach. I dive as fast as I can, but her sword catches my left shoulder as I fall away. I touch the white jacket that I refused to give up for the Rukin one offered to me, and

166

my hand comes away red. I've never broken a bone or gotten stitches or anything, but I don't have time to pass out or freak out because Evora is coming at me again, so I roll out of the way. "Evora, why?!" I shout at her as I run behind a stalactite or stalagmite (the one on the ground, I can't remember which is which). I drop the torch, and everything becomes pitch black.

I see the glow of fire. Evora is using Aveth to see.

"You should have just listened to me, Mia! You should have just learned Aveth." She's looking for me. She doesn't know where I am. I back up behind a shadow.

"This has been the plan the whole time, Mia. The Emperor told me that if I couldn't get you on our side, then I should kill you. Because it would be better to kill you than to let you learn about the Sovereignty."

I can see the light from the fire moving closer to me, and her voice is getting closer. Should I try to run past her? Should I try to fight her? There is no way I can beat Evora in a fight. She's too strong. She's got a sword.

She shoots a blast of fire. And then another. And another, and they're getting closer and closer to where I'm at. She's trying to draw me out. Finally, the blast comes so close to me that my pant leg gets singed as I hurry out of the way. I fall on my injured shoulder and I groan in pain.

Evora has spotted me now and raises her sword again. I back up, but find my back against a stone wall. There is nowhere for me to go.

Faith as small as a mustard seed. Faith as small as a mustard seed.

I see the sword swing down toward me. I close my eyes. I exhale.

I extend my arm and open my hand in Evora's direction.

All of a sudden I feel a force shoot through my hand and it's wind, no, it's Ruach, and Evora flies through the air and lands way on the other side of the cavern. I see her look of shock, and I'm probably making a shocked face too, but there's no time to think about it because I have to get out of here. I can't see anything, so I stumble in the direction I think we came from. I run into walls more than once, and my shoulder really hurts, and it's still bleeding. Finally, I see light up ahead, and I stumble out of the cave.

I have to find Oliver. I have to stop him from closing the portal. I don't even know where the real portal is. I don't even know why they want so badly for him to close it.

Go back to the horses, Mia.

I begin running down the hill, but it's absolute chaos, and I can't concentrate on anything because my shoulder feels like it's on fire. I don't know where I'm going, but I guess I'm going back to the horses, even though I think Vesper and Lucius are back with the horses. I thought I could trust Lucius, though I guess he wanted to kill me all along too, but I don't know what else to do, so I run down the hill, stumbling and rolling more than once, and getting all scratched up along the way.

I make it down to the horses and I see people standing there, but they aren't Lucius or Vesper. The people hear me approaching, and they're wearing white, but so am I, so they don't raise their weapons at me, and then I see that it's Rydan, and Afya, and Bedic.

"Mia!" Afya exclaims.

"Help me!" I shout.

"We were tracking you for days, and we couldn't understand why you ended up here."

"It was a trick." I gasp for breath. "She was going to kill me...because I didn't believe her...Because I didn't use Aveth..."

"Evora?" Rydan asks as he looks back toward the hill. "Is she still up there?"

I nod. "I used Ruach to get away. You were right. I'm so sorry, you were right." And I want to curl up into a ball and I want to start crying, but there is no time because I have to save my brother and I have to stop him from closing that portal.

"You're injured," Bedic notices.

"Please take me to the frozen gate," I say. "I have to stop him. Please help me."

There is a moment of silence where all I can hear is my

panting breath. I think that maybe they won't help me because maybe it's too late, and they still don't trust me, and what if Jayde didn't recover from that bad fall off of the horse when Haston was rescuing me, and what if they blame me for that?

But then Rydan nods curtly and we hop onto the horses.

It takes us forever to get to the real cave with the real portal, but I know we are close when I can hear the sounds of a battle going on.

"We'll clear the way for you," Rydan assures me. Afya and Bedic draw their swords and nod.

"Thank you," I tell them. I wish I had more time with them. I wonder if they really are followers of the True King.

And then, once a path is cleared for me by my three new friends, I run into the cave, hoping and praying that I can reach Oliver in time, before he makes a terrible mistake.

Chapter 18
Study Questions

1. Mia gets a feeling that she is about to step into a bad situation. Where does that feeling come from? Have you ever felt like you should stop doing something you know is wrong? What did you do?

2. The verse Mia remembers is Matthew 17:20. Read it. What is faith? Read Hebrews 1:1-3.

3. What does Ruach represent? How is Mia able to use it? What would this look like in real life?

4. Do you think Mia will be able to stop Oliver in time? Do you think he will believe her? Why or why not?

Chapter 19:
So, the Goalie is a Beautiful Girl
Oliver

You know that moment before you step onto a field before a big soccer game? Every part of your body shakes. Your heart races uncontrollably. There is this excitement that is unexplainable. All the training you've done leads to this moment. Every hour of sweat and pain and practice points to now. This is your moment. You get into place and wait for the sound of that whistle. You stand beside your brothers and your enemies and you can look into each and every face. For a moment, everything slows down, everything freezes. Everyone feels exactly as you do. You're going to win. You have to win. It's all up to you. You can hear the cheering in the bleachers. The sun is beating down on your back. You're so nervous you could throw up, but at the same moment there is nowhere else in the entire world you'd rather be. Then, the whistle blows, and everything explodes into chaos. You're running and kicking and blocking and dodging and diving and fighting and sprinting and waiting and nothing matters but you, the ball, and the guys around you.

So, take all that pressure and multiply it by a gazillion, because this is how I'm feeling right now, crouching here beside Haston, watching the swarm of Kaalinon soldiers guarding the cave entrance. We are squatted behind a big rock, back to back. I can see the frost of my breath as I try to control my breathing. I want to use Aveth to warm myself, but any sound or movement will tell the enemy we are here, and we aren't even ready yet. We want to surprise them. I know that I should feel better with Haston next to me, but there are so many of them, and so few of us. It's like a soccer game, and they have all eleven players, and then it's just me and another guy. Like, we don't even have a goalie. How can we possibly win?

"Now?" I whisper.

"Not yet," Haston bites. And by his tone, I feel like that annoying kid in the back of the car that keeps asking, "Are we there yet?"

I try to swallow, but I'm so nervous, I fail. And if that's ever happened to you before, you know how much it hurts. I'm literally shaking, and I don't wanna be a wuss or anything, but you try going into a battle for life or death with the fate of the world on your shoulders and 167 dudes against two, and tell me how you feel. Yeah. That's what I thought.

"Have any left yet?" I ask. He shakes his head. The plan was that Mia's group would attack first, and it would draw these guys away, but so far, no one has budged. What the heck is Mia doing? She probably found a way to mess this up too. I bet she's doing something weird, like trying to convince the Kaalinon soldiers to hold up signs and protest instead of fight, or something totally unhelpful, and they all got blasted with spears of ice. Then I'm wondering if the Kaalinon soldiers have ice powers. "Do they have ice powers?" He shakes his head again. Come on, Oliver, get it together. Stop being a big baby.

"On the count of three," Haston orders.

What? I'm freaking out! We're going?! How are we going to do this? No soldiers have left! Instead of complaining, I nod bravely, like the champion I am.

"One."

I'm gonna die.

"Two."

It's gonna definitely hurt.

"Three."

I think I black out because the rest is a blur. But I know I'm running after Haston and shouting out my best super-hero battle cry like an idiot and I'm watching Haston blast unsuspecting soldiers away with fire. I extend my hand, think about how awesome I am, and do the same. I can feel the heat coming out of my fingers and I'm seeing guys jump out of the way, like they're side tackling to block a shot, and it's like I have the ball, and I'm moving and weaving through a bunch of dudes, heading to the goal. There are two massive soldiers with spears in front of me. They are wearing white with lame fancy snowflakes on their armor. Not so strong now, are you? They're diving out of the way like all the rest when I shoot Aveth at them. Problem is, four more are behind them, and they're charging me now. I hear shouting from behind. I don't have time to turn around, but you know how you feel like someone is behind you? Yeah. I definitely have people behind me, and they all wanna kill me. What do I do? My favorite spin move that Haston taught me. I call the "Olivernado." Yeah. Lit name, right? So, I'm spinning like a champion, shooting Aveth around me as I do, and they can't touch me. I'm starting to get dizzy, and a path isn't opening up, but at least they can't touch me. I'm still shouting like a maniac, and my Aveth is starting to weaken. This isn't good. As I spin, I can see the look in their eyes and they're all either very impressed or confused. I'm gonna go with impressed. Then, they're screaming and falling, and I stop spinning because no one is looking at me anymore. They are looking everywhere but at me, and then they are starting to run away from other flames. Why? BECAUSE THE SHADIM HAVE ARRIVED!

Listen, I can't explain the joy in my heart, but I'm telling you, like maybe twenty Shadim in golden armor are shooting flames at these ice soldiers and an opening parts for me like it did for Moses at the Red Sea. What? I know my Bible, okay? I listened in Sabbath School. Good kid, remember? I see Haston and he's smiling at me like a proud older brother.

"Go in the cave!" He's shouting at me. "Seal the portal! Now!" He blasts out again. "We'll hold them off!"

I give him thumbs up and do this other move I call the "Shoot-the-Moon-With-Aveth." I mean, it's not an attack or anything; it's more like when Rodrigo makes a goal and then he fires an invisible arrow into the sky. Except mine is way cooler than his because it's *actual* fire and it's real, and yeah, he's got *nothing* on me. My Aveth strengthens again. Still got it. I charge into the cave. I look behind me one last time, and I see the backs of around ten Shadim guarding the cave and fighting to protect me. That's right. *The Ambassador of Elior.* I wonder if after this battle they'll give me a medal or something. I can add it to the two soccer trophies I have at home. Yeah, that's what I'll do.

So, after I'm deeper into the cave, and no one can see me, and the sounds of the battle are kind of far away, I do what any

Aveth-using Ambassador would do. I stop to catch my breath. What? Let's call it a time-out. I'm bending down with my hands on my knees, breathing in and out, praising God I'm not dead. I wonder where Mia is, because this cave doesn't look like it has another opening anywhere, but maybe it will open up farther in. Honestly, I hope she's okay. I hope she doesn't do anything stupid that gets her killed.

I've never wanted my phone or my buds more than this moment. I wish I could put them in and turn on some tunes and get hyped for what I'm about to do. Then I would totally vlog the rest of this adventure. I could show everyone in San Diego what I'm capable of; then I'm sure I'd be a starter this season. Take a seat, Rodrigo. Using a little flame of Aveth, I light up the cave. It's your basic cave. We've seen a lot of them and I'm looking around for something that looks "portaly." They've been calling it the Frozen Gate, so I guess that's what I'm keeping my eye out for. I'm betting that it won't be hard to find, seeing that this cave literally has nothing special to it, just big rocks jutting down from top to bottom, a bunch of frozen puddles, more rocks, and oh yeah, did I mention, some rocks? So, I keep walking through the cave, and now I definitely feel like I'm in every video game ever made, treasure hunting or looking for monsters or something. But Frozen Gates don't attack, right?

The path ahead narrows a bit and the walls hug in closer and I'm glad I'm not claustrophobic like Tracey because she would literally be freaking out right now, and I'm praying there isn't a cave-in today. The path goes up a little, like a small hill, and I'm climbing it. I go higher, wondering what's on the other side, and once I get to the top I stop and look down. The path widens and the walls open back up, the ceiling rises, and then I see it at the bottom of the rocky slope.

The Frozen Gate.

And they weren't wrong. It's like two giant doors made completely of ice. It's as tall as four Olivers standing on top of each other, and the doors are 100% standing open. Next to both icy doors, big bowls hold large flames to light the suddenly giant cave. But the flames don't burn down the doors. It's weird too, because I can't see anything inside the open gate. I squint down into the portal. From up here, it looks like a hazy, fuzzy pool of water, and I can kind of see my reflection and I'm super far away and thin and rippling and buzzing and humming and it's really hard to explain, which is why I wish I had my phone so I could record it, but Mia ruins life. I wonder if I should run down and close it immediately, and then I'm worried the Dark Prince has already come in and he's waiting to clobber me. My heart starts beating again and I can't get my legs to work. It's like the goal is undefended and I have the ball, and everyone is shouting and I'm about to kick it in, and instead I just stop, and I don't know why.

Oh wait. It's not undefended.

The goalie is a girl.

A beautiful girl.

She has long brown hair done in these awesome and confusing braids, icy blue eyes, perfect lips and skin like my color, kinda white, but kinda not. And I'd love to run up and get her number, but she's holding a sword and pointing it at me. I don't want to fight her. I'm a lover, not a fighter, you know? Maybe we can talk about this.

"Hey," I say, casually walking down the hill. I put the Aveth away and give her my best smile.

Let's just say, she's not smiling back. "Not another step," she orders, still pointing that sword at me. The sword is bigger than Haston's. I'm impressed she can hold it with one arm. I'm noticing a silver tiara on her head. She wears sparkly silver armor with a giant snowflake on the breastplate. She has a white cape too.

"Nice cape." What? A little compliment goes a long way. "I like your hair too." Then I notice what's in her other hand. A dagger. A dagger she could easily throw at me. I stop moving and put my hands up.

"I want you to turn around and leave the cave," she orders calmly.

I like her voice. It's deeper and kind of smoky—I dunno how to describe it. Why am I thinking about this? I should just blast the gates closed with Aveth.

"So, can I ask you why you want the Dark Prince to come to Elior?" I ask casually. I'm not turning around, but I'm not moving toward her either.

She carefully studies me and isn't moving at all. "I've heard about you, Oliver," she breathes. "You are strong in Aveth. But my faith is stronger. You will not pass.'"

She's heard about me. Awesome. I'm famous. "What's your name?" I smile again.

"I am princess Aurelia of Kaalinon."

"How old are you?" What? I wanna know! We look the same age.

"Turn around and leave the cave."

"I actually gotta seal it," I mention. "I hope you won't mind."

"You move, I throw." She readies her dagger.

Maybe I should just blast her away with Aveth, but I really don't want to. Ugh, the enemy knows me so well. Guard the gate with a pretty girl I don't wanna hurt. Brilliant plan. Kaalinon 1, Oliver 0.

"Listen, I don't know if you've heard, but the Dark Prince wants to destroy Elior. Tell me why that's good for you, Aurelia. Pretty name. Can I call you Relly?"

"They've been lying to you, Oliver. The Emperor is evil. He calls Prince Kiran the Dark Prince to deceive everyone in Elior. The throne belongs to the Sovereignty and Emperor Zohar stole it from Them."

I think about it. I don't believe her. She's lying to me. Just like Mom did when she told me she'd stay in touch. Like Mom did when I was little, and she told me she'd always be there for me. Like Dad did when he said he'd make it to my games or that tomorrow we'd have a dad-son day, she's lying. And I hate being lied to. "The Emperor is good!" I spit out. "He's trying to save Elior."

"You're ignorant!" She spits out, and for the first time I notice she's shaking. Maybe I can somehow catch her off guard.

"The Emperor can save you too!" I add, taking one step in her direction.

"Stop!" she shouts. "Don't move."

It's now or never. I don't listen. I do the "Olivernado" instead, and spin in her direction. She throws her dagger and dives out of the way. It misses me and I'm twirling toward the gate. I gotta seal it. No matter what. If anything, it's giving Lucius's kid more time. The Emperor is working to find a cure for him. Evora likes me. These people need me. I'm not gonna let a pretty girl distract me from what I've been chosen to do. I hear Aurelia screaming "nooooo" at me, all dramatically, and I get behind one of the open doors and extend my hand, coming out of my spin, and Aveth slams it shut. The entire cave shakes and I'm falling to my knees, and I'm still praying there's no cave-in.

One door left!

I lift my hand into the air.

Nothing happens.

I lift the other one.

I'm frozen there with my hand above my head. I'm starting to freak out, but I can't move them. It feels like a weird wind without any noise is jamming up the Aveth and holding my arms in place. I'm looking around and there's Aurelia, stretching her hands out toward me. Not this again.

"Ruach is stronger, Oliver. Prince Kiran is stronger. One day he will return. And until he does, I will tell everyone the truth about the One True King, and who he *really* is!"

No! Ruach is the anti-Aveth. It's evil! Aveth is good! I have Aveth, and I'm the good guy! This girl is nuts! And I'm struggling against it but I'm failing and sweat is racing down my face. No matter what I do I can't move because of Relly's Ruach. I can't come this close only to fail. Evora is counting on me, Lucius is counting on me, all of Elior is counting on me! I'm still trying to move and I'm still failing, and I can't believe that after all of this, after *everything* that has happened, I choke.

"Oliver!"

I whip my head around and see Haston barreling down the hill toward Relly, aka the ice princess. The thing is, she looks at him too. Closing her eyes and appearing to say a prayer, she takes one of her hands and blasts a gust of wind at him. It literally picks him up and knocks him against the cave wall and now he's not moving. But it bought me a moment. One of my hands is free and I'm shouting again and shooting Aveth at her. She screams as it connects with her arm and I see that I've burned her. I actually *burned* her, and it looks kind of bad. Little tears are coming out of her beautiful blue eyes and I feel really bad but at the same time, don't mess with me. She falls to the ground, holding her arm which opens up the opportunity for me to get to the final open gate. I run to the other side of it and hold out my arm, but there's Mia, standing between me and the gate with her arms fully extended like she's the true goalie, the one that always seems to get in my head. I stop, because I'm not blasting my sister with fire.

"Mia! Move."

"Oliver! Don't do this."

"Honestly, Mia, now is not the time to be some weirdo with a cause."

"Evora tried to kill me."

Wait, what? *"What?"*

"Look at me! I'm *bleeding*! Evora tried to kill me!"

"What are you talking about?"

"EVORA TRIED TO KILL ME! IT'S NOT COMPLI-CATED! SHE'S EVIL! SHE STABBED ME!"

"Yo, stop talking stupid, just because I have a girl-"

"LISTEN TO ME!" Now she's talking fast, and I've never seen her like this. I'm wondering how she got here so sneakily. Hand it to Mia, she's like a weird purple-haired mouse. Never see her coming. Wish she'd go away. "Evora has been lying to you this whole time. The Emperor is evil; Prince Kiran is good. You're helping the bad guys. Don't seal that gate!"

But I don't have time to listen to this nonsense. I know Mia. I know she would say whatever she needs to say in order to get me to look stupid. Yes, she has some *red* around her shoulder area, but I wouldn't put it past Mia to like spread berry juice on herself or a tomato or something. Also, I have Haston's voice ringing in my head. He warned me this would happen. When they captured Mia, they filled her head with a bunch of lies. He told me they would turn her against me. It's literally happening. Besides, I *know* Lucius is good. Yelling at her won't help the situation, so, I'll have to take a different approach. I speak slowly and calmly. "Listen, I don't know what you thought you saw with Evora, or what those freaks did to you when they had you, but remember, we were brought here for a reason. They saved us in the forest. You were tied up! You were captured! You're not thinking straight!"

"I can't believe you'd listen to your dumb girlfriend over me!"

"They brainwashed you! We gotta close it, Mia! Move!" And like the Flash, I dash. I pounce at her. I'm way faster. Way stronger. Way cooler. I don't blast the doors this time. I leap toward her, pushing her out of the way, and simply touch the door with Aveth. Everything starts to shake, and the door starts to close super slowly and super dramatically. I swear the cave is shaking like it's the biggest earthquake I've ever seen. And trust me, I'm from California. I know my earthquakes.

But I remember Mia is fast too. She leaps up and moves around the closing door toward the open portal. I laugh to myself. What is she going to do? Stop the door from moving with her shrimpy body? This I have to see. "Come on, Mia. Move out of the way." She raises her arms. Why?

Then, time seems to slow, and my heart drops. I see Haston, and he's charging Mia from behind. His sword is high up in the air, and he's literally about to chop my sister in half. No. Not Mia. Not my sister. What is he doing?!

No way.

Could she be right?

No. There must be some sort of confusion. There must be a reason, right?

What is he doing?!

Haston is too strong. Too quick. Too powerful. If I blast Aveth at him, I'll hit them both, so I start to bolt in their direction, but something crazy happens. Out of the corner of my eye, I see beautiful Relly, burned arm and everything, extend her hand in Mia's direction. Suddenly, right as Haston's sword is slashing down at Mia, she gets lifted away and up above Haston's head with Aurelia's Ruach. The princess nods, then flicks her hand, and sends Mia through the portal.

"Nooo!" I scream! I think this girl just sent Mia to the

Dark Prince's lair! But wait, if Haston really tried to kill Mia, where could this portal actually lead if maybe they were lying all along? Or was Haston simply willing to sacrifice Mia in order to stop the Dark Prince from returning? I mean, she was about to try to stop the portal from closing, right? All these thoughts slam through my head as the door continues to shut and everything is shaking violently, and I'm staring into the portal, looking at my reflection.

There I stand. Just a kid, really. At my core, I'm like everyone else. Terrified of life, not sure how to live it, just doing my best. So stupidly selfish. I'm not enough, not really. Not enough for Mom, not enough for Dad. I feel like no one really loves me, so I guess I love myself too much. Aveth has me drained, and I'm wondering now if I should have used it. I feel sick. I feel empty. I want to throw up. I'm just not enough. I try to be more, but I fail a lot. The truth is, I don't really know who I am, and maybe that's why I can't ever tell who is lying and who is telling the truth. All I know is that Mia is gone, and the door is about to shut away forever. Evora tried to kill Mia? Haston tried to kill Mia? I look at Aurelia and our eyes meet, and she looks scared for me. I look over and Haston is towering above me. His eyes are burning with hatred and rage and I'm terrified. I hear the door scraping shut behind me. The shaking intensifies.

"Thank you for your service. The Emperor sends his regards. Remember—he is the one true king," he sneers, and he shoves me through the portal as the door slams shut.

Chapter 20:
So, When the Time Comes
Mia

It's dark and I find myself flying through the air. There's not enough time to worry about where I'm going to land or if I'm going to land because almost immediately, I hit the hard ground.

"Ow…" I sit up and reach for my injured shoulder.

Except it isn't injured anymore.

And there isn't any blood.

AND I'M WEARING MY SWEATSHIRT!

I realize I'm wearing my normal, same clothes that I was wearing when we first went through the waterfall. I'm shaking because a second ago Haston was about to run me through, and now I don't even know where I am or what's going on, but I realize I can see, and that I'm still in a cave, but the entrance isn't very far away.

I scramble to my feet and run to the entrance, heart pounding. Where am I? Where did that portal drop me?

The opening to the cave is kind of narrow, and I have to turn sideways to get through it. I begin pushing my way through when I hear a groan behind me. I jolt around and find Oliver laying on the ground in the same place I was just a minute ago.

"Oliver!"

He's holding his head and his eyes are closed. I rush over to him. "Are you okay?"

His eyes flutter open. "Mia? Mia!" He frantically sits up and wraps his arms around me. "Are *you* okay?" Oliver's eyes are full of fear.

"Not now," I tell him. "I mean later, yes, we need to talk about this, but first we need to figure out where we are and if we're safe." I don't think I need to remind him that last time this happened we fell literally into a battle. I mean I don't *think* we've landed in the Dark Prince's lair, but that doesn't mean this is a good place.

Oliver pats his pocket and pulls out his phone. His eyes get ten times bigger. "Woah. No. Way. MY PHONE!" And he's literally jumping up and down and I'm thinking we have bigger fish to fry at the moment. I shake my head. "Do you have service?" I ask.

He shows me. It says "Roaming."

I snatch his phone out of his hands and pull up Google Maps. "It says we're in...Abisko...SWEDEN?!"

"In...in *our* world?"

I show him the map. We're in a national park. In our world.

"The portal led back to our world?" Oliver asks, confused.

"We gotta call Mami," I realize. She's probably been worried sick. She probably thinks we got kidnapped by serial killers. I pull Oliver out of the cave with me.

I take out my phone and dial Mami's number. Oliver stops me. "Isn't that gonna cost a lot of money?"

"Who cares?!" I say louder than I mean to. He doesn't answer, so I press call and wait for Mami to answer.

"*Bueno?*" Mami answers casually as if her children haven't been missing for who knows how long.

"Mami, *estamos seguros*," I say quickly. We're safe. We're alive.

"Huh?" she asks. "Is something wrong?"

I look at Oliver. "What day is it?" I whisper to him.

He looks at his phone. "June 18? Wait, isn't that…"

"The same day we left," I finish. We stare at each other for a moment. Has, like, no time gone by?

"Mia? *Que esta pasando?*" I hear Mami's voice on the phone.

"Uh...okay, hear me out," I begin. "So...we're in Sweden..."

"Ha ha, very funny. I just saw you a second ago. Where are you?"

"Mami, I'm not playing, look at my location on your phone..."

I wait a few seconds while she looks. "WHAT?! You were just here! You're in SWEDEN?! *Ay dios mio! No puede hacer!*" She screams so loudly that I have to pull the speaker away from my ear.

"Look, I can explain, but, um, what do we do right now?" Because I'm kind of freaking out. And, also, I'm actually not sure I can explain this.

"Okay, just stay where you're at, I'm...hang on." I hear mumbling in the background. I think that's Lito's voice. "You what?" Mami says, and everything else is muffled. I look at Oliver and shrug. Soon, her voice comes back clearly. "Okay, apparently Lito knows someone in the area you're in? Don't ask me. But he will message her on Facebook and see if she can pick you up. Is there a safe place you can go where there are adults while we, I don't know, book a flight, I guess?" Now she's properly freaking out.

"Uh...I don't know..." I look around. The scenery is beautiful, I think. It's pretty dark out, but the stars are bright. There's a small brook nearby. But I don't see any people or buildings.

Mami stays on the line while we look for the nearest place we can go. It turns out there's a visitor's center for the Abisko National Park a couple miles away. I look at my phone and see that it's 9:14 PM, and I'm guessing it's closed by now. We promise to tell her as soon as we get there. She promises to make sure someone will keep us safe until they arrive. I guess we'll hang out in the parking lot or something.

Meanwhile, Oliver and I don't really know what to say to each other. We arrive at the visitor's center and sit on a bench outside. Oliver is shaking. I'm not doing much better, and I don't know what to say to help him.

"Okay, but maybe there was a misunderstanding" Oliver says, his leg tapping restlessly.

"Are you kidding me? Evora and Haston tried to kill me, Oliver, and you saw one of them try!"

"But you don't know for sure that he was aiming for you." I start to argue with his ignorant statement, but Oliver cuts me off, saying, "And there's no way Evora would ever try to hurt you. And she wouldn't lie to me. There's gotta be something else going on here. Maybe they ate poisonous mushrooms or something."

I stare at him like he's sprouted three more heads. "Do you hear yourself? Look around, Oliver, the portal brought us *home*. Well, sort of. This sure isn't the Dark Prince's lair."

"Maybe they were confused," Oliver says. That's all he's willing to admit.

"You're unbelievable." I cross my arms and lean back against the bench.

Before long, a tan car pulls up right in front of us, and an old woman gets out. She looks at the two of us. "Mia? Oliver?"

We nod.

She points to herself. "Kristina." Kristina has short gray hair, and she walks with a cane. She doesn't speak English, but she talks to us anyway, and shows us Lito's Facebook profile picture. She points to the passenger side door and asks us a question.

"We're not supposed to talk to strangers," Oliver tells her. As if she understands him. I make a quick call to Mami, confirm that this is Lito's friend, and she tells me that Lito is on the way to the airport right now. I wonder how on earth Lito is friends with this ancient lady who has a million wrinkles. What are the odds he's connected to someone in Sweden? In this area? Who could come pick us up? RANDOM.

We are with Kristina for about a full night and a full day. During that day, Oliver and I argue again about what exactly happened at the frozen gate. At least both of us are positive we didn't just, like, have a weird lucid dream. The fact that we're currently in Sweden takes away that option for doubt.

"His name is Prince Kiran," I tell Oliver. "He's not dark.

He's not evil. He's the True King."

"You don't have proof," Oliver insists. "How could you possibly know for sure that the Emperor is bad? All you know is what they've told you."

I shake my head. "It's more than that." I open my journal to the front cover and read to him: "'For this very reason, make every effort to add to your faith goodness; and to goodness, knowledge; and to knowledge, self-control; and to self-control, perseverance; and to perseverance, godliness; and to godliness, mutual affection; and to mutual affection, love.'"

"What does that have to do with anything?"

"Those are the qualities a person who follows Jesus tries to have. It's the same thing with Prince Kiran. Maybe they're the same. I don't know. I still have a lot of questions."

Oliver sighs, and says, "You don't even know the Bible like I do, Mia. When was the last time you went to church? If anyone would recognize the True King, it would be me."

"Seems like a dangerous thing to assume," I murmur.

"Let's just figure out how we're going to explain this to Grandpa," Oliver snaps.

Something dawns on me. Oliver gasps. We look at each other. "Estrellita!" we both exclaim at the same time.

Great. Now we have to explain to Lito that, not only have we spent weeks in another world, but, oh yeah, also we lost his dog.

In a whirlwind, Lito shows up at Kristina's house. They share a conversation using Google Translate, Lito gives us our passports, and we fly back to Michigan where Mami is probably waiting to skin us with *la chancla.*

Lito doesn't ask for an explanation. He's a little upset about Estrellita, but he shockingly takes it in stride. He is very quiet for the whole 14-hour flight.

We land in Houghton County Memorial Airport, which is about a four-hour drive from Paradise. We're exhausted at this point, but Lito parks at a cafe on the way and ushers us inside.

"Okay," I begin once I've gotten a croissant and hot chocolate. We are sitting at a booth in this quaint little cafe and there are only two other people in here. "Can I just say that I am so sorry about…"

"Mia," Lito holds up his hand. "I'm the one who owes you an explanation. Both of you. Please listen to me."

Oliver and I look at each other, then back at Lito. "We're listening," I say.

He nods and takes a sip of his tea. "In the beginning, the seven kingdoms of Elior were created. A portal was placed in each except the High Kingdom."

My mouth drops open. "Lito, what…"

"What is happening?" Oliver asks.

Lito holds up his hand again. "Let me continue," he says.

I mean, what else are we going to do?

So, he goes on. "Many years ago, my mother, your great-grandmother Zoila, was the first Ambassador to go through the waterfall portal in Canterbor. Her family had moved to Wisconsin. They were just visiting when she came across it."

"Are you serious?" I gasp.

"Why else would I know this?" Lito questions. Good point, Lito. Good point.

"My mother discovered that the portals had been created by the Sovereignty. We know them here as the Father, the Son, and the Holy Spirit. But in Elior, they are the High King, the High Queen, and the High Prince."

I stare daggers at Oliver. I knew it. I knew this was somehow related. Oliver is busy staring at his folded hands.

"The Ambassadors were sent from our land to Elior to share the truth about God between both places. Each portal has a location here and in Elior. You just came through the one in Sweden."

"And Kristina?" I ask. "Was she an Ambassador too, then?"

Lito nods. "Very good, Mia. Yes, Kristina was great friends with Abuelita Zoila. She even went to her funeral."

"This is crazy," I shake my head.

"During her time there, my mother witnessed something known as the Great War. It was when the Sovereignty's closest advisor rebelled against them. He took a third of the kingdoms with him as well. That's when the Blight started."

The Blight. Something I've heard about before. "The Blight. It's what's killing Elior, isn't it?"

Lito agrees. "Yes. But your great-grandmother was so strong. She fought for good alongside the king of Canterbor. She was an amazing force for light." Then, his smile turns to a frown. "But once she returned back through the waterfall, she was unable to ever get back to Elior. She found out later from Kristina that the Sovereignty's advisor had crowned himself Emperor and had all six of the portals closed."

I look over at Oliver. It's pretty clear to me now that the Emperor is bad, especially based on what I saw with my own eyes. But Oliver has been super quiet through this whole thing, and I wonder if he still doesn't believe me and if he still thinks that Evora is one of the good guys.

"I grew up with these stories," Lito says. "It's why our family always came back to the area. Why we still live here. I always hoped to be able to go through the portal...but it remained closed. At least, it was closed last time I tried. All I know is, our family has a special connection to Elior. It is no surprise to me that you are both Ambassadors."

I lean forward. My turn. I tell him everything we know. About how there's a revolution going on against the Emperor. How Canterbor and Kaalinon were able to get their portals open. How Oliver and I were tricked into closing the one in Kaalinon.

How we need to go back and fix what we broke.

Oliver says nothing. He's lost in his own head, I guess. I want to know what he thinks of all this, but I'm afraid to ask him.

Lito agrees to drive straight to the campsite where we found the waterfall. He makes sure I have our passports in my backpack just in case, you know, we end up in another country again. And he agrees to help us explain everything to Mami if we want. Did I mention how awesome my abuelo is?

187

So, here we stand, Oliver and I, shoulder to shoulder, staring at the waterfall in front of us. The place where all this crazy stuff started. And we have to go back to fix things. At least, that's why I want to go back. Oliver hasn't really said anything, but he did agree to go back with me, so that's something at least. He'll see once we get there. He'll realize what I realized.

I take a deep breath and lead the way.

We push through the water and my hair gets wet. My clothes get soaked. It's super dark, and I get ready for the sudden daylight that I know waits for us on the other side. I take one step, then another. I'm coming, Prince Kiran. I'm coming back to help your loyal followers.

I run face first into hard stone. "Ow!" I jump back, holding my nose.

Oliver turns on the flashlight on his phone. Sure enough, the waterfall is behind us, but instead of that forest in Elior we're face to face with the back of the waterfall.

"Oh, no," I say, touching different parts of the wall, looking for a secret passageway or something. "No, no, no, no, no. It has to be here. It has to be here."

Oliver's face is pale. He grabs my arm. "Mia, stop. It's closed. This one's closed, too."

My heart is beating quickly. "But...but we have to go back. They need our help."

"It's closed." Oliver is frowning and looking kind of angry, and I just can't figure out what's going through his head.

But I know for sure that this is really, really bad. Lito said the job of the Ambassadors was to share the truth in our world and in Elior. Well, we royally messed up in Elior. And I desperately want to get back there to fix it.

In the meantime, though, what do I do here? How can I keep living the way I've been living when I know now that the Bible is real? When I know that there are people who are literally willing to die for the God they believe in?

We go back through the waterfall, and I sit down right there on the grass. I have so much to think about. "It's all real," I whisper.

My number one goal is to return to Elior somehow, some way, and help get rid of the Emperor once and for all. But, for now, I'm going to do some digging for myself. I'm going to learn how to fight. I'm going to learn everything I can in the Bible.

So, when the time comes, and I can return once again through the waterfall, I'll be ready.

You bet I'll be ready.

Chapter 19 and 20 Study Questions

1. Why does Oliver still not believe the truth? What could be holding him back?

2. Mia's faith starts small, and yet is powerful enough to defeat the enemy. What enables her faith to grow?

3. Mia and Oliver never resolved their issues with each other. Why not? What could have gone differently if they had reconciled?

4. Why do you think Oliver and Mia were unable to go back into Elior?

5. Reread Hebrews 11. How does faith make a difference in our relationships with each other?

6. Who do you think is the True King?

Mia and Oliver will return in
The Ambassadors of Elior and
the Dual Thrones.

Find more books and information at
enspireproductions.org/books

Glossary:

Afya: Canterbor soldier, is a teenager

Aurelia: princess of Kaalinon

Aveth: the power that comes from having faith in the Emperor and in oneself

Bedic: Kaalinon soldier, has a handlebar mustache

Canterbor: one of the seven kingdoms of Elior, the forest kingdom, the kingdom's official color is green and its sigil is a tree, set south of Rukin, rebelling against the Emperor

Cerise: Rukin soldier, is a mother

Courtney: Oliver's girlfriend in San Diego

Dark Prince: former ruler of Elior

Edie: Kaalinon soldier

Elior: has seven kingdoms, the land in which Oliver and Mia discover through a portal behind a waterfall

Emperor Zohar: current ruler of Elior

Estrellita: Oliver and Mia's grandparents' caramel colored pom terrier, called "Pluto" by Oliver

Evora: princess of Rukin, daughter to Jethil

Haston: a powerful Shadim

Horn Terror: ferocious ten-horned beast found in the deserts of Rukin

Jai: Rukin soldier, becomes friends with Oliver

Jayde: Canterbor soldier, right hand woman to Rydan

Jethil: King of the desert kingdom of Rukin

Kaalinon: one of the seven kingdoms of Elior, the ice kingdom, the kingdom's official color is white and its sigil is a snowflake, set in the far north, rebelling against the Emperor

Kessia: wife to Lucius

Linnetia: Rukin soldier, really likes Estrellita

Lucius: Rukin soldier, is Princess Evora's bodyguard, father to Vyn and husband to Kessia

Malek: elite members of the Dark Prince's army

Odynne: crown princess of Rukin, daughter to Jethil, sister to Evora

Ralik: Rukin soldier, has an intellectual disability

Rodrigo: Oliver's friend from San Diego

Rukin: one of the seven kingdoms of Elior, the desert kingdom, the kingdom's official color is orange and its sigil is a sun, set south of Kaalinon and north of Canterbor, loyal to the Emperor

Rydan: Canterbor soldier, has a scar on his face

Shadim: elite members of the Emperor's army

Tracey: Oliver's stepmother

Vesper: a powerful Shadim

Vyn: Lucius's terminally ill son

Zoey: Oliver's stepsister

About the Authors

Devin Anavitarte has worked at Burton Adventist Academy in Arlington, TX since 2013. He currently serves as the campus Chaplain and Bible teacher. Co-author of The Shepherds of Oldaem series, Devin has also written 24 plays. With an M.Div. from Andrews University and a Bachelor of English from Southwestern Adventist University, Devin enjoys swimming laps, playing tennis, playing games with friends, and writing.

A native of Keene, Texas, Stephanie Wilczynski has an M.A. in English from Andrews University and is currently pursuing a Ph.D. She is very passionate about youth ministry, spending many years working at summer camps and as co-author of the Shepherds of Oldaem series. Stephanie lives in Dallas, Texas with her husband and best friend, Jonny, where she is a teacher at Burton Adventist Academy.